PROFESSING ROMANCE

A ROMANTIC COMEDY

R.H. JOHNSON

Copyright © 2022 R.H. Johnson

ISBN 9798445160328

Published by Hampton, Westbrook Publishing, Princeton Junction, New Jersey.

This is a work of fiction. Names, characters, businesses, places, events, and incidents are either the products of the author's imagination or are used in a fictitious manner. Any resemblance to actual persons, living or dead, or to actual events is purely coincidental.

First Edition

Cover image: Filmovar/Shutterstock.com

Book layout by www.ebooklaunch.com

OTHER BOOKS BY R.H. JOHNSON

Widow-Taker, 2015

A Measure of Revenge, 2016

Hunting in the Zoo, 2016

The Kirov Wolf, 2017

Eyes in the Cave, 2017

Sailing the Gates of Hell, 2018

The Charleston Assassin, 2018

Hollow-Point Diplomacy, 2019

The Jericho Option, 2019

The Bermuda Terror, 2019

The China Mandate, 2020

Fear River, 2020

Mountains Will Fall, 2020

Sanibel Bones, 2021

The Moscow Initiative, 2021

The Virgo Paradox, 2021

Rain in Dark Woods, 2022

Books written as Alastair Flythe

Noblest Love, 2018

King of the Vultures, 2018

Two roads diverged in a wood, and I—
I took the one less traveled by,
And that has made all the difference.

Robert Frost, "The Road Not Taken"

1.

Mating season arrived unannounced shortly before noon on April 10th when Hickston College welcomed its first ninety-degree day of the spring semester. No starting gun sounded and no siren wailed, but every student on campus felt the powerful hormonal surge. A warm, inviting breeze washed over the school's lush two-hundred-acre hilltop campus, and the games began.

Walking from the faculty parking lot toward his office in Caterwaul Hall, Assistant Professor of English Grant Hunter was struck by the startling change in scenery. On the previous day, spring's tentative signals had been limited to a few songbirds flitting among the Japanese cherry blossoms and to mounds of golden forsythia cascading over the campus walks. Today, however, the landscape featured young women in outfits only slightly less revealing than the average Australian bikini and by young men partially covered by jogging shorts and threadbare T-shirts.

A phrase popped uninvited into his head. *April, dressed in all his trim, hath put a spirit of youth in everything.* He could not remember ever having memorized the line, yet there it was after all these years, clear evidence that Shakespeare had indeed been an astute observer of the world around him.

Two coeds walked out of the bookstore as he approached, and one of them, Elissa Palfrey, smiled sweetly and wiggled her fingers at him in a coquettish wave. Tall and lithe with flowing blond hair that caressed her bare shoulders, she wore a ruffled crop top that exposed several inches of slender waist above the tiniest pair of faded cut-off jeans he had ever seen. She had been cute, he recalled, when she had sat in the front row of his freshman English class several years earlier, but now as a senior she was cover-model gorgeous and without question the most striking woman on campus. As she swayed toward the library with her friend, Grant couldn't help but notice the way she filled out her almost nonexistent shorts.

"Falling in lust, are we?" came a voice from behind.

Grant turned toward his accuser and was relieved to find his friend Jim McArdle grinning at him. Jim was chairman of the math department as well as an energetic basketball player who played lunchtime pick-up games with Grant at the gym two or three times each week.

"I was simply waving to a former student," Grant protested.

"A beautiful former student, as it turns out, and one who could probably be arrested for wearing those shorts," Jim laughed. "Can I offer a word of advice?"

"Do I have a choice?"

"No, you don't. Be a little more discreet about studying the female form while you're still up for tenure."

"Yeah, you're probably right. Where are you headed?"

"Lunch. Care to join me?"

"I have a 1:00 o'clock class, so I'd have to make it quick."

"Quicker is always better when Vulture Commons is involved."

The college had rebranded its dining hall in honor of the school's mascot two years earlier, right after the men's basketball team had shocked the sports world by capturing the NCAA championship. The name change had not, however, affected the quality of the culinary experience. Students regularly argued that no self-respecting vulture would eat what passed as food in the commons, and the weekly campus newspaper had a regular column devoted to complaints about bloody chicken, mushy vegetables, and two-thousand-calorie fatburgers. But since Vulture Commons was the only place on campus to obtain a hot meal, the place was always busy.

Faculty members were usually well represented at the commons at lunchtime since the twenty-minute drive into town was overly inconvenient. Beyond that, the local community didn't have much to offer aspiring gourmets. The top-rated eatery on Main Street was Margot's Grill, a much-maligned hole in the wall where the daily special was always shepherd's pie except on Thanksgiving Day, when turkey chili made a brief appearance on the menu. After Margot's came Shen's Chinese Pizzeria, where no Hickston faculty member had ever dined. Even poorly paid professors had their standards.

Following a long wait on the cafeteria line—students had recently begun calling it the Vulture Death March—Grant ordered beef stew instead of a grilled cheese sandwich paired with soggy fries. It turned out to be a bad choice. After one spoonful he pulled what at first glance appeared to be a brown fish bone from his mouth and held it up for closer examination.

"It's a bristle from a pot brush," Jim volunteered in between bites of his burnt sandwich. "I found thirteen of them in the stew yesterday."

"You had the stew yesterday and didn't tell me about the bristles?"

"I assumed it was new stew."

"How in God's name do they manage to get four-inch bristles in beef stew?"

"I'm not a chemist, but I assume that if you accidentally drop a large brush in a vat of stew," Jim replied, "boiling does the rest." He thought for a moment then added, "I swallowed one of the bristles yesterday, and I'm still alive. So they're probably not toxic."

"Good to know."

They applied themselves wordlessly to their meals for a few minutes, but Jim finally pushed his unfinished sandwich aside, covered the remains with a paper napkin, and said, "Have you heard anything about the tenure decision yet?"

"Not a word, and I don't know whether that's good or bad."

"Probably good," Jim lied. He would be sad to see his friend leave Hickston College, but it seemed inevitable.

"Here's hoping," Grant said without conviction.

He had submitted his thick tenure package—resume, personal statement, and other required items—back in October after beginning his sixth year on the Hickston faculty, and this was his one and only shot at becoming a permanent member of the English department. The school's policy was clear and inviolable: faculty members who didn't attain tenure by the end of six years were given the boot.

If granted tenure, he'd be promoted from assistant professor to associate professor and have a secure position for the remainder of his career. If he was turned down, well, the outcome was too grim to contemplate. He was already forty-four, five years past the average age at which college faculty members earn tenure, and he didn't have the stomach to endure this process again.

Grant Hunter was a man without options.

2.

Grant's 1:00 p.m. class, *Writing Short Fiction II,* was held in a cramped, airless room on the top floor of Pawling Hall, more commonly referred to as Appalling Hall. The grotesque three-story brick structure, built in 1907, had been allowed to fall into disrepair. Chunks of plaster fell without warning from its ceilings and exploded in clouds of white dust on the decrepit wood floors. Leaky lead pipes frequently failed, transforming large sections of wall into a gooey, oatmealish substance that smelled faintly of dead mice. And, naturally, like other buildings of its vintage, the place had no air conditioning.

Windows on the first two floors of Pawling Hall could sometimes be opened with herculean effort, assuming a member of the school's football team happened to be in the classroom, and this allowed a bit of fresh air to circulate on the hottest days. Windows on the third floor, however, had been painted shut decades earlier and would never open again. So it was a foregone conclusion that Grant and his students were doomed to suffer throughout the session. But he would suffer the most because he had to find something positive to say about the awful short stories his students had turned in the previous week.

Words like *wretched, imbecilic,* and *juvenile* came to mind, but he couldn't use them. Like non-tenured instructors everywhere, he lived constantly with the threat of social media and grade-the-professor websites that could easily upend his career. Although the dean of faculty claimed not to give any weight to an instructor's online ratings, everyone knew he did. There was, in fact, a well-documented correlation between low student ratings and swift terminations. Since tuition and fees covered more than ninety percent of Hickston's bills, the college adhered to an unwritten "the customer is always right" policy that forced faculty members like Grant to choose between maintaining academic standards and shamelessly currying student favor.

Grant understood the game and played it remarkably well. To begin with, he looked like someone students could trust. Handsome but not excessively so, he had fashionably long brown hair, a winning smile, and a pleasant manner. He also kept himself quite fit, and at six-foot-one, one hundred and eighty pounds could still hold his own on the basketball court. Most important, though, he knew what he could and could not say to students in order to keep his online ratings at the top end of the range. His score on the most frequently used rate-the-prof site was a perfect five, making him one of the most popular teachers on campus. He was almost universally considered a cool guy and a soft touch when it came to grades.

His friend Jim, on the other hand, had a rating slightly below two because his math classes were ridiculously difficult and because getting an A from him required divine intervention. But Jim neither knew nor cared what his online rating was since he had tenure and was therefore on the faculty for good unless he raped or murdered someone. And he was hardly that kind of guy.

"I'm going to read for you a couple of sentences from one of the short stories you turned in last week," Grant said with as much energy as he could muster in the sweltering heat, "and I want you to tell me what you think."

He unconsciously ran the side of his hand across his sweaty forehead. The temperature in the classroom was approaching one hundred but felt even warmer because of the stale air. Six of his eleven students did their best to pay attention despite the horrific conditions, two dozed, and three devoted themselves to texting.

Grant began reading. *She loved the beach best. She spread her old blue blanket on the sand and was like, I could stay here forever. But then she was like, no, I really can't because I have like a ton of stuff to do. So she went in the water and then drove home.*

"Okay," he said. "Comments, please."

He hoped someone would notice how the word *like* was being used as a pathetic form of punctuation that had no place in serious conversation or writing. Or how a childish phrase like *a ton of stuff* could be upgraded with a few seconds of additional thought. Or how the person in the short story would not likely go into the water and then drive home unless she had a remarkably versatile automobile.

"I like the description of the blanket," one young man announced, proud to have contributed to his final grade. "*Old blue blanket* is a lot better than, like, just *a blanket*."

Two students nodded in agreement while one more nodded off. Grant felt numb. Had his students not listened to anything he had said since the first day of class?

"You can feel the conflict," a young woman in the front row chimed in. She slowly crossed her long, bare legs, watching Grant's eyes follow her as she did so. She figured she was a lock for an A. "She's, like, torn over what she should do."

Grant fantasized anew about his idea for slap therapy. Each time one of his students punctuated a sentence with the word *like*, he would slap him or her until the message finally sank in. The word had become meaningless junk, a sloppy yawn as unnecessary to effective communication as scratching one's butt to signify the end of a sentence. But here in the real world he had long ago thrown in the towel. Even some of his fellow professors had begun filling the vacant spaces between their thoughts with *like*, and he had bigger battles to fight.

Getting tenure was at the top of the list.

Yes, his student ratings were excellent, and he knew that would count for something. But his academic credentials were somewhat anemic. A Pennsylvania native, he had earned a B.A. from Lebanon Valley College followed by an M.F.A. in creative writing from the University of New Hampshire. He had then spent seven years teaching freshman composition classes at a community college before moving on to a series of temporary faculty positions at four-year colleges in New Hampshire, Maine, and Vermont.

While other junior faculty members were publishing pretentious academic papers and toiling away on their doctorates, Grant devoted himself to writing the great American novel. As far as he was concerned, teaching was nothing more than a way to pay the bills until he became a famous author. Once the royalties began flowing, he would ditch the academic career and live happily ever after turning out book after book.

But his first novel, *Infectious Memories*, had come to an abrupt end after two months and eight chapters when he realized he had nothing much to say about anything of consequence. One of his M.F.A. professors had warned him this would be the case, declaring that the best writers were those who had lived long enough to have opinions and observations worth sharing with their readers. Young Grant had nothing but dreams of his own success, and that left him roughly ninety thousand words short of a novel.

Chastened by this early failure, he began writing short stories. After all, he told himself, writers as famous as James Joyce, Katherine Anne Porter, and John Updike had burnished their reputations with collections of brilliant short stories, so why couldn't he do the same? Almost all of his stories dealt with sports or campus life, the only two things he actually knew anything about, and he found them easy to produce. After cranking out thirty-one of them, he began looking for a literary agent. Eighteen rejections later, he decided to self-publish the collection through Amazon. He rationalized the move by telling friends that self-publishing meant he wouldn't have to share his sales revenue with agents, editors, or publishing houses. It was a flimsy argument, but it was the only one he had other than the truth: making it as a writer was next to impossible.

He titled the book *Infectious Memories and Other Short Stories.* The first and longest story of the collection was, naturally enough, "Infectious Memories," the dusted-off remnant of his abandoned novel. Like all the other stories in the collection, it was a modestly insightful coming-of-age tale in which a young man gained valuable insights into issues like self-reliance, perseverance, and loyalty. The writing was confident and crisp throughout, and Grant managed to avoid most of the clichés that usually haunt young writers.

The book was well received by fifty-two readers, forty-one of whom had purchased the Kindle edition for ninety-nine cents. It was, in other words, an inauspicious beginning. But then fortune chose to smile upon the fledgling author. One of Grant's few readers happened to be the arts editor of the *Steinville Courier*, a weekly newspaper serving Steinville, New York, a charming, old-fashioned town situated on the Hudson River Palisades about six miles south of Highland Falls. She wrote a glowing review in which she used the word *adore* seven times, and the piece got noticed by Hickston College's human resources manager, who at that moment happened to be searching frantically for a creative writing teacher who would also teach several sections of freshman composition. Because the new academic year was set to begin in less than three weeks, she was desperate.

Grant was desperate as well, having recently departed the latest of his numerous temporary teaching positions, this one in Bangor, Maine. After snagging the Hickston position, he packed his meager belongings, drove seven hours to Steinville, and moved into a tiny studio apartment located three miles from campus. He had heard of the college only because of its star basketball player, Winston Churchill Mbongo, who had powered the Hickston Vultures to two consecutive national championships. Grant realized that basketball was probably more important than academics at Hickston, but he could not have cared less. The one-year contract would cover rent, utilities, and food, leaving a little something for whatever constituted social life in Steinville.

Six years later he was still gainfully employed, but the clock was racing toward the all-important tenure decision. This was make-or-break time, and his only ace in the hole was the English department chairperson, Professor Hannah Grackle, who had vowed she would vigorously support his tenure application.

She was all he had going for him.

3.

Hannah Grackle hated Grant. She couldn't quite put her finger on why, but she did.

Maybe it was his youthful good looks and exuberance. Since she was fifty-eight, frumpy, and as charming as a gravestone, she had a natural aversion to people who reminded her of all the things she was not. The difference between two human beings could hardly have been greater.

Or maybe it was that students loved him but signed up for her courses only when absolutely necessary. The reason for this was fairly obvious. Pretty coeds and star athletes could usually count on getting an A or B from Grant, while the worst student in the class would get at least a C as long as he or she showed up regularly for class. Grackle, on the other hand, was an unrelenting taskmaster who took a sick delight in pouring on the homework and publicly humiliating students who disappointed her in any way. Over the past twenty-three years only four students, all female and all English majors, had gotten an A in one of her courses.

Or maybe it was simply because she had glowing academic credentials—among them two published books on Old English poetry and more than a hundred scholarly articles—while Grant had nothing on his resume other than a self-published collection of short stories and a pitiable list of temporary teaching positions at what she considered disreputable institutions. She found it offensive that he carried the title of assistant professor with so little substance behind it.

Grant had not been her choice. She had been hiking the Inca Trail in Peru with a private tour company at the time the English department's former creative writing professor quit at the last minute. Because the new academic year was close to beginning and Grackle was unreachable, Hickston's HR manager had pulled the trigger on Grant. Not doing so would have meant canceling all the creative writing classes that dozens of students had signed up for as well as shifting nearly one hundred freshmen to other composition instructors. The potential for lost revenue and angry students made the decision a no-brainer, especially in light of the college's habitually precarious finances. But the move had infuriated Grackle when she finally got word of it in her room at Gringo Bill's Hotel in Machu Picchu. Sadly for her, the fury she unleashed on the HR manager changed nothing. Grant had already been given a contract and would serve as a member of the Hickston faculty.

The exhausting twenty-five-hour journey from Peru to Steinville—a trek incorporating a bus, a train, a donkey, two Boeing 767s, and more mini bottles of scotch than she could remember—had given Grackle ample time to read *Infectious Memories and Other Short Stories* on her Kindle. She loathed everything, beginning with the subject matter. Since she had no use for college sports, highly paid coaches, or entitled jocks, it was hardly surprising that she found Grant's stories about the glories of athletics to be the stuff of nightmares. Reading them was like continually being poked in the eye with a sharp stick.

Even worse, in her estimation, was the writing. She considered his hip, breezy, conversational style an affront to good taste. Having spent her entire academic career steeping herself in the history of the English language and mastering communication theory, she felt that exposing someone like Grant to Hickston's students was comparable to bringing a stray mongrel to the Westminster Kennel Club dog show. It simply wasn't done.

Yet it had been done.

Following this initial setback, Grackle had twice tried and failed to have Grant's year-to-year contract terminated, but Dean of Faculty Byron Shuttleworth had overruled her both times, arguing that Grant's stellar online ratings and low salary were a perfect combination. Grant's achievements as an author and scholar were virtually nonexistent, Shuttleworth freely admitted, but students liked him and claimed to have learned something in his classes. So the dean was not about to ignore the wishes of satisfied customers. Grant would stay, and Grackle would have to deal with it.

Deal with it she did, but in the style of a veteran politician. In order to placate the dean, she hid her hostility toward Grant behind smiles and kind words, promising him that she would speak on his behalf in front of the tenure committee, which she served as vice chair. But in the meantime she made sure he taught the worst classes at the worst hours and in the worst classrooms. He thought it was simply bad luck that he always had an 8:00 a.m. class on Monday and a 6:00 p.m. class on Friday, but that's because he didn't understand how the system worked. Grackle always had an opportunity to review class schedules before they were released, and she saw to it that Grant had to be on campus both early and late five days a week. Since she also had the final say over what classrooms were assigned to each course, she made certain that Grant practically owned the third floor of Pawling Hall. This, too, he chalked up to bad luck rather than sadistic manipulation.

Grant's friends knew only too well that his chief character flaw was a rather naive willingness to take people at face value. He seemed not to have learned how to distinguish between friend and foe.

Grackle was getting ready to teach him.

4.

On the way back to his office after the one o'clock class, Grant ran into Tex Brawner, head basketball coach and currently one of the most famous sports figures in America. Once a struggling NBA assistant coach, Brawner had led the Hickston Vultures to two consecutive national championships over perennial powerhouses like Duke, Kansas, and Gonzaga, and most experts believed he had a strong shot at four consecutive titles thanks to the young man walking alongside him.

Though Brawner stood six-four and carried slightly more than two hundred pounds on his well-built frame, he was dwarfed by Winston Churchill Mbongo, the seven-foot-eight, three-hundred-pound all All-American center who was widely regarded as the best basketball player on the planet, either amateur or professional. Winston could handle the ball like a point guard, rain jump shots from anywhere on the court, and look down into the basket while dunking. Every pro team in the world wanted to throw money at him, but Winston intended to be the first man from Nimbe, his village in Cameroon, to earn a college degree. Despite his incredible basketball skills, he proudly considered himself a student first, an athlete second.

And this made Tex Brawner one of the luckiest men alive.

"Good afternoon to you, Professor Hunter," Winston said joyously. He had already gotten four A's from Grant—two in freshman comp and two in creative writing—and was about to get a fifth in *History of the Novel*. Winston wrapped his huge hand around Grant's and shook vigorously, though not so vigorously as to break any bones.

"And good afternoon to you, Winston. Hi, Tex. What are you guys up to on this fine spring day?"

"We just finished showing a five-star recruit around campus," Tex answered. "He's six-ten and moves like a cat. He'll make a great power forward."

"Think you can get him?"

Tex grinned. "Yeah, he's coming. He just wanted to make sure Winston wasn't jumping to the NBA."

"I shall be here for two more years," Winston said emphatically. "I will be a bachelor of the sciences. Then one day I will become a doctor and serve the people of Nimbe."

A biology major, Winston had straight A's in all of his science courses and nothing below a B in any other subject. Whether he would play in the NBA for a few years after graduating or go directly to med school was a subject he hadn't addressed yet. He was thoroughly enjoying his time as a Hickston student and was in no hurry to move on.

"How are things with you, Grant?" Tex asked. The two had grown close over the past few years even though they worked different sides of the campus, and Tex was well aware that a committee of faculty elders would soon rule on his friend's future.

"Still sweating out the tenure decision. If I don't make it, I hope you'll throw me a couple of tickets now and then."

"I've got you covered on the tickets, but let's not worry about the other thing until you get the final word."

Grant had been an early and highly vocal supporter of Hickston's fine young coach, and he happened to be one of the few academics who believed Tex's two-million-dollar salary was money well spent. Faculty elitists were outraged that a basketball coach earned ten times more than a full professor even though it was the basketball team, not Hickston's mediocre curriculum, that kept the admissions staff employed.

"Yeah, you're right," Grant said half-heartedly. "The word should be coming down any day now. Grackle says she'll be pushing for me."

Pushing you off the nearest cliff, Tex said to himself. He had run into Grackle during his first year at the college, when she had helped lead a movement to have Hickston drop all intercollegiate sports. He would not forget or forgive how she had gone about trying to bring him down. Posing as one of his avid supporters, she had used the false friendship to learn something, anything, that might help get him fired. In the end she had succeeded only in getting herself on the extremely short list of Tex's archenemies. Her day would come, but until then he kept his thoughts on Grackle to himself.

"Come on over and shoot some baskets," Tex suggested.

"I'd love to, but I have an office hour from 2:00 to 3:00."

"You really think someone is going to drop in on a day like this?"

Grant shook his head sadly. "Not a chance. But if someone does show up and I'm not there, that's the sort of thing the tenure committee could use against me."

Tex and Winston walked off, and Grant continued toward Caterwaul Hall. He followed a shady path that ran the length of the woodsy campus, stopping briefly to smell the lilacs that bloomed in great abundance alongside Haught House, the 1904 colonial where the alumni director and his staff maintained offices. A workman in blue overalls stood on a stepladder repairing a broken first-floor window, the casualty of a boozy weekend alumni reception during which a member of the class of 1967 had relived the old days by throwing an empty beer bottle across the room. It was one of the hazards of bringing aged fraternity members and alcohol together on a college campus.

Before reaching his office, Grant passed Castle Cliff, a steep, grassy overlook where students frequently admired the Hudson River while giving free rein to their hormonal urges on warm spring nights. He noticed a pair of liplocked lovers on one of the two wooden benches and immediately felt a twinge of regret. Spring and all its delights were operating at full throttle, yet he was alone, still waiting for the perfect woman to come his way. It could hardly be otherwise, of course. He taught all day and wrote all night. How was he going to find someone?

His last serious relationship, meaning one that had survived for more than a month, had come and gone during his junior year of college. After that he had dated occasionally without finding anyone capable of holding his interest. He often wondered whether it had been him or them. He sometimes accused himself of overthinking a relatively straightforward process that had led most of his friends, male and female, to the altar shortly after graduation. On the other hand, more than half of his happily married friends were now even more happily divorced, so perhaps his foot-dragging had been a blessing in disguise.

Still, he found it mildly disconcerting that his love life had essentially hit a wall. The only women he dated these days, and rarely at that, were other faculty members, mostly devoted geeks whose idea of a good time was attending a rousing lecture on Martian microbial fossils or the restoration of Mayan ruins in some half-forgotten Mexican jungle.

At the same time, though, he recognized it was probably better this way since a serious relationship would only complicate life now that he teetered on the precipice of career ruin. He already lived from check to check on his meager assistant professor's salary and might have to wait tables or sell insurance if the tenure committee ruled against him.

Why would any woman of sound mind want to share his misery?

5.

Grant's fourth-floor office was small, dark, and cluttered. A decrepit wooden desk, marred by the use and abuse of an untold number of temporary faculty members over the years, held several neat piles of student papers and a stack of unread campus mail. On one wall a long bookshelf sagged under the weight of yellowed textbooks that had collected dust there since 1921, the year Caterwaul Hall opened. Standing alongside the opposite wall was a cheap lamp table Grant had rescued from a dumpster behind his apartment building. The table held a coffee mug, an immersion heater, a plastic jar of instant coffee, and a brownish metal spoon on permanent loan from the dining hall.

The creaky swivel chair behind his desk faced the room's only window, one so dirty that even direct sunlight could barely penetrate its ancient layers of soot, grime, and seagull droppings. He had complained endlessly about the window's condition since taking possession of the office six years earlier, and each time he had been assured that the project was definitely on the maintenance department's to-do list. But the job required suspended scaffolding, and that meant having to hire an outside company. So the estimated completion date, currently July 2025, kept getting pushed back.

Grant was on the phone deleting voicemails and didn't realize he had a visitor until she softly cleared her throat. He turned to find Juliet Swanson, Hickston's most recent homecoming queen, smiling seductively from the doorway. She was a raven-haired beauty who would no doubt look stunning in a burlap sack and combat boots. But today she wore a considerably more alluring ensemble: a tight white spaghetti strap tank top along with filmy pale-blue short shorts and expensive blue-and-white Nike running shoes. The first word that popped into Grant's head was *goddess*. The second was *trouble*.

Juliet was not simply another Hickston student. She was one of Grant's students, and she had blithely violated his extremely generous unwritten rule: just attend class if you want a C. Because she had rarely attended class throughout the spring semester and had flunked every exam so far, she was doomed. The best she could hope for was a D, and even that would be an early Christmas gift.

"Do you have time to see me, Professor Hunter?" she asked invitingly. She seemed to pause slightly over the words *see me*.

This was not the first time he had noticed her perfect full lips, now shimmering under sheer gloss. But since she had never spoken in class, he hadn't been sure that her lips were actually capable of forming words. He suddenly found himself wondering whether the words she had spoken had been intentionally provocative or had simply been misunderstood.

"Of course." He smiled and gestured toward the wobbly chair next to his desk.

She approached like a tigress about to bring down an unsuspecting antelope. Heeding Jim McArdle's advice, Grant kept his eyes focused on her face, but his peripheral vision captured the elegant motion of her flawlessly proportioned hips. She sat, casually brushed a few careless strands of hair from her face, and leaned closer, studying him with haunting silver eyes that left him slightly breathless.

"Professor Hunter," she said with a sexy pout, "is there anything I can do to get an A in your class?"

She locked eyes with him, a cobra hypnotizing a doomed mouse, and he was unable to look away despite the obvious danger. For a moment he had the eerie sensation of leaving his body and floating above the room on the subtle jasmine scent of her Armani perfume. Part of him wanted to tell her that yes, in fact, there was a way for her to get an A in his class. But his brain remained in full control of his senses, reminding him that Juliet Swanson had TERMINATED FOR CAUSE written all over her.

"I assume you're aware that right now you've got a pretty solid F locked up," he said.

"Uh, huh. That's why I'm here." She began playing with the delicate gold choker that adorned her long, slender neck. "I thought if I could, you know, maybe get some private tutoring, I still might be able to get an A."

"We've covered five novels this semester. Have you read all of them?"

"Not yet. But I'm going to start this afternoon."

Grant nodded. "Well, that would be a good start. Tell you what. We have another three weeks of classes before the final exam. If you read all the novels, attend every single class, and get an A on the final exam, you might be able to get a B for the semester."

"There must be something I can do to get an A, Professor Hunter." The sexy pout returned. "Isn't there?"

"It's simple math at this point. The final exam counts for one-third of the grade, so it can't possibly offset all the grades you've gotten so far. But if you knock the ball out of the park over the next three weeks, you might—and I emphasize the word *might*—be able to get a B. And obviously that's a lot better than a D or F, right?"

"An A would be better," she purred.

His defenses were on the brink of crumbling when a bold voice from the hallway saved him.

"The faculty meeting is in twenty minutes," declared Georgette Mealey, Grant's seventy-year-old English department colleague. She had served as the department chairperson ten years earlier and still tried to keep people on their toes. "Are you heading over?"

"Yes, absolutely. I'll walk with you." Then to Juliet, "Read the novels, attend every class, and ace the final exam. Then I'll see what I can do."

They stood at the same time, and their faces nearly touched. She parted her lips slightly, as though inviting a kiss, then smiled and thanked him for his help. She left the office convinced she would get an A for the course. The final details of the arrangement could be worked out later.

"When I was in college," Georgette whispered to Grant as she watched Juliet glide down the corridor, "girls weren't allowed to dress like prostitutes on campus."

"I really hadn't noticed," he managed to say with a straight face. "I guess it's the style."

"A trashy style, if you ask me."

Grant didn't respond. He was too busy wondering what it was about Juliet that had finally gotten to him. Was it the pout, the purr, the perfume, or those haunting eyes? Whatever it was, for a few minutes she had made him feel twenty again.

And what a dangerous feeling it was.

18

6.

Short, plump Arthur Sproull might have been walking to the gallows instead of to the president's office. No condemned man had ever moved more reluctantly toward his destination, each slow step reflecting his dread of what awaited him. He knew that if he didn't pull a rabbit out of a hat by the time the academic year ended, he would become Hickston's *former* vice president for development. He was a chief fundraiser who hadn't raised nearly enough funds to satisfy President Porter Farnsworth, and his career was on life support.

Sproull's expensive Brooks Brothers suit failed to hide his weak knees from Sarah Townsend, the president's secretary. She knew him to be a windbag who had survived on big talk, unfulfilled promises, and pure, unadulterated dumb luck during his Hickston career, and she looked forward to seeing him walk out the door for the last time. She also knew the end was near. Sproull had less than a month to reach the twenty-million-dollar fundraising goal that President Farnsworth had set, and he was more than seventeen million dollars short.

"He's waiting for you," Sarah said blandly without looking up from the letter she was typing. She cruelly added, "And he's in the mood for some good news."

The grilled cheese sandwich Sproull had eaten for lunch rose to the back of his throat, but he successfully gagged it down.

"Yes, well, we have several extremely large gifts on the way," he proclaimed in his deep, officious voice. "I'm sure he'll be pleased with the progress we've made."

She stifled a laugh. Unless Sproull had brought with him a gigantic check made out to Hickston College, something she seriously doubted, he was about to be eviscerated by the man in charge. Farnsworth was in as foul a mood as she had ever seen.

Sproull knocked twice and opened the door to the president's palatial office, a sprawling domain where oversized windows offered spectacular views of the Hudson River, virgin forestland, and even the towers of distant New York City on especially clear days. Farnsworth was seated at his enormous mahogany desk poring over the college's latest financial summary.

"Good afternoon, Porter."

"Is it?" Farnsworth snapped. "According to the March-end numbers, we're going to run a seventeen-million-dollar deficit for the year. So please tell me how that makes this a good afternoon."

He rose from his desk, thrust the financial document at Sproull, and waited for an answer. Farnsworth was an imposing figure, tall and stout with a mane of white hair that lent him a regal air. As always, he wore a custom-made navy-blue suit, one of seven that hung in his closet. Today's blue suit was accompanied by a monogrammed dress shirt with French cuffs and a handmade burgundy silk tie. He was arguably one of the best-dressed college presidents in America thanks to the "President's Discretion" line in the Hickston budget. Not once during his seven years as president had he been forced to spend his own money on expensive clothing, hair styling, or spa treatments. Since he believed that looking successful was simply part of the job, he had no second thoughts about letting the college pay the full tab for his grooming.

"I didn't mean to suggest it's literally a good afternoon," Sproull replied meekly. "I was just being polite."

"I don't need politeness. I need money. *A lot* of money. And I need it fast. And you," he jabbed Sproull's chest with his index finger, "are the person who's overpaid to bring the money in."

"We're on the brink . . ."

Farnsworth cut him short. "And if you dare tell me we're on the brink of a bombshell gift but don't have a fat check in your hand, I may be forced to strangle you. I've heard your tall tales about bombshell gifts before, Arthur. What I want today is for you to tell me how much money is coming in and when."

Sproull had endured some rough meetings with the president over the years, but this was the first time the word *strangle* had found its way into the conversation. Farnsworth's crimson face and wide eyes made the possibility of homicide seem all too real.

Sproull took a deep breath to steady himself. "I was about to say we're on the brink of some very good news. Beatrice Hagfeldt has stage-four pancreatic cancer and is receiving hospice care at home." He couldn't help but smile. "I saw her yesterday, and she looks absolutely terrible."

Over the years he had earned the nickname Sproull the Ghoul for the devoted attention he gave dying benefactors, and in most instances his instincts had proved correct. Only once had a major donor disappointed him by cheating the undertaker.

"How long and how much?" the president asked, momentarily placated.

"Two weeks, give or take, according to the doctor. And forty million dollars given today's stock price for Curetell Sciences."

Farnsworth smiled. "That much?"

Sproull nodded. "The stock has been skyrocketing lately because Curetell is rumored to have developed a vaccine that is nearly one hundred percent effective against most forms of cancer."

"Please don't tell me it can cure pancreatic cancer."

"No, no, no. Beatrice is finished, Porter. The vaccine prevents but doesn't cure."

"Thank God for small favors. And her doctor, you believe him when he says she has only two weeks left?"

"He hungers to become a member of Hickston's board of trustees," Sproull noted, "and would never give me bad information. She has two weeks at most. For all we know, she could go tonight. And we're in the will for everything: the Curetell stock, the bank accounts, the house, and the dog."

Farnsworth scowled. "No way we're keeping her dog."

"Of course not, Porter. It will be in a shelter before her body is cold."

Sarah Townsend knocked once and entered the room. She seemed disappointed not to find Sproull's entrails scattered about the floor.

"Dean Shuttleworth is on the phone," she told the president, "and he needs to speak with you right away."

"I'll call him back."

"Unfortunately, he needs you to chair today's faculty meeting, which begins in about ten minutes."

Farnsworth had never been good at hiding his anger, and the thought of having to preside over a faculty meeting triggered a magnitude 9.0 earthquake. He snatched the phone from his desk.

"Byron, I hate faculty meetings. You know that. What's going on?"

The dean's coughing fit offered a clue. When he finally recovered, he spoke in a raspy, halting voice that kept breaking up because of a bad cell phone connection.

"I'm sick . . . flu, in bed with . . . one hundred and two . . . chills."

Farnsworth imagined himself a World War II spy attempting to decode an enemy message. But he got the gist of it. His dean of faculty was sick with the flu and wanted the president to take his place.

"For God's sake, you have a dozen deans, associate deans, and assistant deans," Farnsworth complained. "Why can't one of them cover the meeting?"

Shuttleworth waited for another bout of coughing to subside. "Can't . . . tenure announcements . . . important."

"So I have to be the one to announce the new tenured professors, is that what you're saying?"

"Yes."

"Then give me the names."

Through intermittent coughing Shuttleworth managed to say, "All eligible faculty . . . fortunately . . . approved. Cheryl has . . . list."

Farnsworth angrily checked his watch. "Fine, Byron. I'm on my way. But never stick me with one of your meetings again. I have a college to run." He hung up and turned to Sproull. "I want that old biddy dead, Arthur. We need her money yesterday."

"There's not much I can do to speed things up, Porter."

"Listen to me. I don't care whether you pray, put the evil eye on her, or stick pins in voodoo dolls. She's no good to us alive."

The president stormed out of his office, leaving Sproull to wonder whether he had just been ordered to murder Beatrice Hagfeldt. The thought was repugnant. On the other hand, he really needed this job.

Besides, she was going to die soon anyway, wasn't she?

7.

Miranda Davignon stood in the shade of a maple tree next to Latten Hall, an austere stone conference center built in 1942, and popped a breath mint when she saw Grant approaching. She turned to a window and quickly checked her reflection to confirm that everything was in order. It was. Her caramel hair showed off a new pixie cut that perfectly framed her lovely, delicate features. The bright floral top and beige cotton slacks she wore were appropriate for both the weather and the occasion. *Intelligently perky* is the look she had aimed for, and she had hit the bullseye.

Miranda was forty-one, six months removed from an unpleasant divorce, and still hopeful of finding her life partner. Though she and Grant had never dated, they had chatted now and then in the dining hall or at faculty gatherings, and he had invariably struck her as a gentle sort whose style lined up nicely with hers. He never pretended to know more than everyone else in the room, always gave his full attention to the person he was speaking with, and had an easy, casual manner that made people feel comfortable. In short, he was almost the polar opposite of every other man on campus.

She glanced at her watch. The faculty meeting would begin in another seven minutes, and she wished he would walk a little faster. But, then, he was keeping pace with Georgette Mealey, who had stopped walking fast twenty years earlier, and Miranda considered that one more thing to like about him. He was considerate of others and not at all embarrassed to be seen strolling across campus with a hobbled old woman nearly twice his age. Most younger male professors wouldn't be caught dead in the company of someone like Georgette, but Grant seemed totally unaffected by the opinions of shallow people.

Georgette headed straight for the ladies' room when she entered Latten Hall while Grant went over to a buffet table, which was always the highlight of faculty meetings. Unfortunately, the trays of freshly baked chocolate chip cookies had already been picked clean by the early arrivals, most of them junior instructors whose salaries barely covered simple necessities like food, but he managed to grab one of the few remaining bottles of Evian. He unscrewed the cap and took a long drink.

"*Eau de France*," Miranda said as she moved next to him. "*Parfait.*"

Grant turned and smiled when he saw who it was even though the language had given him a strong clue. Miranda was a full professor of French—tenured, naturally—as well as chair of the foreign languages department. He had first met her during his second year on the Hickston faculty.

"Water from France," he translated. "Perfect."

"You get an A."

"Actually, I got a low C in high school French, so I switched to Latin. But even an incompetent like me understands *eau* and *parfait*. Hot day, isn't it?"

"Yes, unusually hot for this early in the season, but I've always loved spring. It's my favorite season, although I like autumn almost as much."

He nodded. "Those are also my two favorite seasons. In fact, I'd be happy to divide the year between them and skip summer and winter completely."

"Summer is fine if I'm traveling," she said, "but I've never been someone who enjoys sitting in the sun and baking for hours on end."

"Do you and your husband have any big travel plans this summer?"

Mystery solved. She now knew why Grant had never shown any interest in her.

She smiled and shook her head. "My ex and I got divorced last fall."

"Oh, I hadn't heard." Unsure of whether to extend condolences or congratulations, he simply said, "I guess we should go inside."

She nodded, and they walked together into the large lecture hall and took adjoining seats. As they did so, they caught the tail end of a conversation between the two female assistant professors who sat behind them.

"Are you sure?" one of them asked nervously.

"I heard it from one of the associate deans. Shuttleworth will announce the new tenure names today."

"How many?"

"No idea. I guess we'll find out shortly."

"Good luck to us, then."

"Amen."

Miranda spoke over Grant's right shoulder. "Aren't you up for tenure this year?"

"I am, and I have my fingers crossed. If I don't get it, I'm toast." He immediately pictured himself flat broke and living in his car, assuming he could still afford a car.

"I've seen your online ratings, Grant. Students love you. That counts for a lot."

"But I suddenly wish I had written a bunch of boring academic papers instead of short stories. I'd probably have a much better chance."

She surprised him by saying, "I've read your short stories, and I think they're wonderful. There's certainly room on this faculty for both creative writers and scholars, so you get my vote."

"I graciously accept. Hannah Grackle also said she'll support me, and that should help."

The meeting was called to order before Miranda could tell Grant she would never turn her back on Grackle, who during her time at Hickston had skillfully trashed the careers of numerous talented instructors. In Miranda's view, this was Grackle's way of sustaining departmental mediocrity so that her own star, dim though it might be, could shine the brightest.

Professor Olaf Schotz, chairman of the faculty senate, cleared his throat loudly, waited for everyone to settle down, and then announced that Dean Shuttleworth was bedridden with the flu and thus could not attend the extremely important meeting. His words were met with enormous glee. No one in the room would miss Shuttleworth's grating voice and his wearisome tendency to drone on about inconsequential matters.

The mood quickly swung in the opposite direction, however, when Schotz announced that the president would be taking Shuttleworth's place. Faculty members were willing to tolerate Farnsworth as long as he stuck to cultivating major donors and making sure Hickston's bills got paid. But on those rare occasions when he ventured onto their turf, they bristled at the thought of a man with a Ph.D. in recreation management presuming to guide their deliberations on academic matters.

Farnsworth strode magisterially to the podium, offered tepid thanks to Schotz for the tepid introduction, then spent the next twenty minutes holding forth on some of the year's major achievements. The notably short list included the basketball team's second consecutive NCAA championship, a brass plaque from the New York Society of Commercial Architects for the restoration of the oldest dormitory on campus, and a certificate of merit from Steinville Mayor Charles Dinwoody for the school's modest contributions to the local community.

Annoyed by the sea of glazed eyes and stifled yawns that stretched before him, Farnsworth suddenly blurted, "And I am pleased to report that we are in the final stages of receiving a bequest of more than forty million dollars."

A rifle shot could not have had a more shocking impact on the audience. The standing ovation that followed Farnsworth's announcement was by far the grandest he had ever received, and he basked in the glow of his triumph. Since the college's endowment was presently only six million dollars and shrinking, everyone in the room knew what such a huge gift would do for the school's financial health. Among other things, it meant that long-overdue faculty raises would almost certainly be in the offing.

It was a great day for Hickston College.

Now all Farnsworth needed was for old Beatrice Hagfeldt to die on schedule, and he was highly confident in that regard.

Sproull the Ghoul had a keen nose for death.

8.

Farnsworth smiled and held up his hands, signaling for quiet. When the faculty members finally stopped clapping and sat, he moved on to the next topic, one he knew was guaranteed to trigger additional applause.

"There's more. Right before coming here, I spoke with Dean Shuttleworth, and he shared with me some wonderful news." He paused for effect and surveyed the silent room. Every eye was on him. "All faculty members who were up for tenure this year have been approved. I would like those people to stand and be recognized."

The cheering began immediately, and the six faculty members whose careers had just been given the tenure committee's official seal of approval gratefully accepted the congratulations of their colleagues. By far the happiest person in the room was Grant, who accepted a brief congratulatory hug from Miranda.

"I knew you would get it," she whispered. "I couldn't be happier for you." She squeezed his forearm to reinforce the message.

"Last announcement of the day," Farnsworth said when he decided the backslapping and handshaking had gone on long enough. "In the adjoining room you'll find drinks and hors d'oeuvres in honor of our new tenured faculty members. Please come and celebrate the occasion."

Not wishing to get trampled, he remained at the podium as the faculty stampeded into the banquet room for the rare treat of food and booze on Hickston's tab. He could not have been more pleased to see everyone in such a fine mood. Everyone, that is, except Grackle, whose crimson face and death glare suggested she had murder on her mind.

Farnsworth had done battle with Grackle on several occasions and had no desire to do so again anytime soon. So when she rose from her chair and began coming for him, he turned and retreated to the banquet

27

room. She almost followed him but stopped short when she saw him near the doorway shaking hands with Grant, who had already gulped down half a glass of chardonnay and was standing next to Miranda Davignon. Deciding this was not the proper setting for World War III, she left Latten Hall and marched toward Dean Shuttleworth's office.

"How does it feel to know you have a permanent home at Hickston?" Farnsworth asked as he snagged a mini mushroom quiche from a passing tray.

"Stupendous," Grant replied. "I honestly wasn't expecting it, and I still feel a bit overwhelmed."

Farnsworth clapped him on the shoulder, then wandered into the crowd to extend his good wishes to the other guests of honor. A waiter bearing a tray of bacon-wrapped scallops took the president's place. Miranda took one, and Grant took three.

"You know," Miranda said between dainty bites, "maybe I shouldn't say this, but I was really worried when you told me Hannah Grackle had said she was fully behind you on the tenure issue."

Grant seemed surprised. "Why's that?"

"Well, she has been known to undermine more careers than she's boosted, so I had my doubts. I'm relieved she did something good for a change."

"Something *really* good. I'll be promoted to associate professor, which means my salary will go up, which means I'll be able to move out of the shoebox apartment I've been living in. With a little luck, I might actually be able to buy a house for the first time."

"Have you looked at any homes?"

He shook his head. "It made no sense to look unless I got tenure, but I guess the time has finally come."

"If you need help looking, let me know. I'm familiar with most Steinville neighborhoods and can steer you toward the best ones."

"I'd really like that."

She flashed her brightest smile. "So would I."

Slightly giddy from the wine as well as Miranda's kindness, Grant asked whether she would join him later that evening for a celebratory dinner at a lovely restaurant he knew of up in Highland Falls. She had to decline the invitation because she would be attending a 6:00 p.m.

meeting of the Steinville Town Council, to which she had been elected three years earlier. It was an unpaid position but one that allowed her to play a key role in revitalizing Steinville's business district, schools, and real estate market. She was an energetic community leader as well as a respected academician.

"When I get home tonight," she said, "I'll check out some property listings online, and maybe we can look at a few homes this weekend. If you have nothing else planned, I mean."

"I'll have to reschedule doing some laundry and vacuuming the living room," he joked, "but otherwise my weekend is wide open."

A man who does laundry and knows how to use a vacuum cleaner! Miranda was much impressed. Her ex-husband had been shocked to learn that a woman doesn't actually long to clean the house and cook three meals a day while holding down a full-time job.

She handed her half-finished glass of wine to a waiter and told Grant she needed to leave for her meeting.

"What's the hot topic tonight?"

"A zoning variance that would allow a big-box store to open its doors in Steinville and destroy Main Street."

"I hope you vote no."

"Oh, trust me. This won't happen while I'm on the council."

He believed her. She struck him as someone who was accustomed to making things turn out her way.

As he watched her leave the crowded room, he had the odd sensation of having dreamt everything: the tenure announcement, the president's personal good wishes, and happy colleagues all around him. But if it was a dream, he didn't want it to end.

Life had never been better.

9.

Campus prudes considered it scandalous that Farnsworth shared his opulent presidential home with Alicia Fillip, widow of the former dean of faculty. But neither Farnsworth nor his live-in lover seemed to care what anyone thought. They enjoyed each other's company, had no desire to get married, and were consenting adults. So they lived openly and happily in the Georgian mansion that sat at the eastern edge of the campus.

The magnificent stone edifice had been built there in 1910 by Ogden Vandermeer, a Dutch immigrant who had made a fortune in banking before being sentenced to thirty years in federal prison for bank fraud. Following Vandermeer's incarceration, Riverview College of the Liberal Arts, later renamed Hickston College, purchased the mansion and its ten-acre plot at auction for five hundred dollars, roughly equivalent to fourteen thousand dollars in 2022 dollars. The roof leaked occasionally above one of the six bedrooms, and the basement had standing water in it year round, but the home was otherwise an architectural treasure that had served presidents and their families for nearly one hundred years.

At 8:00 p.m. Farnsworth was in his favorite leather recliner sipping Bowmore single malt scotch and bemoaning the fact that the five-hundred-dollar bottle was nearly empty. It had been a prized Christmas gift from one of Hickston's largest vendors, but in retrospect he realized the gift had been only half as generous as it might have been. He wondered whether it would be terribly improper to drop hints about receiving a second bottle prior to December. A July Fourth gift, for instance.

This required further thought.

He was greatly displeased when the cell phone interrupted his deliberations and Byron Shuttleworth's name popped up on the caller ID. For the dean of faculty to call a president at his home was, in

Farnsworth's view, a ghastly breach of protocol unless the world was coming to an end, which clearly it was not. He was tempted to let voicemail take over. Then he considered the possibility that it was actually Shuttleworth's wife calling to say that her husband had died. The dean *had* sounded awful that afternoon. Farnsworth imagined what a huge inconvenience it would be to find a replacement dean since truly qualified candidates demanded far more compensation than Hickston's budget could bear.

"Farnsworth here."

"It's Byron."

"So my telephone says. You're sounding better."

"I'm feeling a bit better."

"And you called me at home to tell me this?"

"No." A long, uncomfortable pause followed. "We have a problem. You announced at today's faculty meeting that everyone who was up for tenure had been approved."

"Because that's what you told me. I have an exceptional memory, Byron. You said that all eligible faculty members had fortunately been approved. Then you told me to get the list from your secretary, but I saw no reason to get the list since *everyone* had been approved."

"No, Porter, what I said was all eligible faculty *except, unfortunately, Grant Hunter,* were approved. That's why I wanted you to have the list."

"Well, your message would have been far less garbled," Farnsworth said snidely, "if you hadn't been coughing and choking the entire time. But in any event, *we* don't have a problem. *You* have a problem. You screwed this up, so you can fix it. Goodnight."

Farnsworth settled back in his recliner and poured himself another two fingers of Bowmore while Shuttleworth frantically paced his bedroom, ugly visions of Hannah Grackle swirling before him in the dim light. Immediately following the faculty meeting she had raced to his office prepared to drink the blood of whoever had approved Grant for tenure even though the committee had turned him down at her insistence. Since Shuttleworth hadn't been there at the time, she had raged at his secretary until Cheryl, near tears, produced the official tenure list to prove that the committee's wishes had indeed been honored.

31

"Then get Dean Shuttleworth on the phone," Grackle had snarled, "and tell him to clean this mess up fast. The committee's decision stands. Grant Hunter is history."

Lacey Shuttleworth had taken Cheryl's call and promised to pass the message along to her sick husband as soon as he woke up from his highly medicated nap. Then she had raced off to her evening Pilates class and didn't return to their small campus home until 7:45, when she dutifully delivered the bad news.

The dean had felt himself on the mend until he heard about the bungled announcement. His fever and body aches were then quickly joined by a bout of severe nausea. At the very least, the fiasco would be massively embarrassing for everyone involved, especially Grant. At the other end of the damage spectrum was the lawsuit Grant might file for the emotional distress caused by Farnsworth's screwup. It was a horrible situation either way, and Shuttleworth had hoped to hand the problem off to the man who had caused it.

He should have known Farnsworth wouldn't let that happen. The president was infinitely skilled at taking credit for victories and giving full credit for defeats to his staff, and he would certainly let Shuttleworth swing from a lonely branch.

"So what are you going to do?" Lacey asked as she wriggled out of her hot-pink spandex bodysuit for the second time in two hours. The first time she had gotten a helping hand from her Pilates instructor, thirty-year-old Lars Jonassen.

"I'm torn between slitting Farnsworth's throat and slitting my own."

"Would you like me to break the tie?"

"Very funny."

Lacey grinned playfully, but she was only half-joking. There were times when she believed a large life-insurance settlement would be preferable to spending the rest of her life with a stodgy, overweight academic—a man eighteen years her senior, no less—who ruled a lackluster faculty at a mediocre college. If it weren't for her Pilates sessions, she'd feel old even though she was only fifty-one.

"Seriously, what will you do?" she persisted.

"Tonight, nothing. This isn't something I can handle over the phone. Tomorrow morning, sick or not, I'll have to go to the campus and find Grant and hope he's not feeling homicidal."

32

That makes one of us, Lacey thought. She left him to brood over the crisis and strolled nude toward the bathroom for a long bubble bath.

"You might want to pull the shades down when you walk around like that," he muttered.

"Why? Do you think there's someone on campus who hasn't seen a woman without clothes on?"

"I assume you mean a woman other than you."

She smiled wantonly and did a slow three-sixty. Shuttleworth shook his head in dismay, wondering once again why he had fallen in love with this younger woman.

Then he remembered. She was miraculously oversexed.

10.

Grant reached his dreary monk's cell of an office at 7:15 a.m. to pick up handouts for his first class, and he paused at the doorway to study the place. The threadbare rug. The pinkish-gray dust blanketing everything that hadn't been touched recently. The mummified mouse that had lain under the bookcase since the day he moved in.

For six years he had tried not to notice how shabby and unfit the room was because it was the space he had been assigned. And, naturally, as a junior untenured member of the faculty, he had been in no position to demand something more presentable. But those days were nearly at an end.

He wouldn't need to request a more suitable office because it came automatically with tenure and the promotion to associate professor. His new windows would be large and, with luck, would look out on the heart of the campus rather than on the battered dumpster that had taken up permanent residence behind Caterwaul Hall. The furnishings would be cleaner, newer, and more befitting someone of his status. He would no longer be embarrassed to have colleagues and students stop by.

He pictured himself at his new desk adding clever phrases to the outline for his next novel. Once the outline was finished, he would take a one-year sabbatical to write at his leisure in some inspiring location. Maine, perhaps, near a lighthouse by the sea. Or maybe a small Key West cottage, close to where Hemingway had done some of his best work. But he would return to campus now and then to show his face and trade pleasantries with admiring colleagues. When they asked how the book was coming along, he might toss out tantalizing bits of the plot. He would enjoy long dinners and much intelligent conversation with his peers. He would grow a sensible beard and take up a pipe.

First things first, of course. He had lectures to give, tests to administer, and papers to grade. Not until the spring semester officially ended could he turn his full attention to writing. In the meantime, he would begin looking seriously at homes in the area. With Miranda's help, he would find something charming and suitable. It would have a comfortable study, ideally one with a fireplace. A spare bedroom, in case his parents came to visit. And a private, well-shaded backyard with a Weber grill.

He had paid his dues and was about to reap the rewards. Life, it seemed, was fair after all.

A nasally voice from behind interrupted his reverie.

"Hello, Grant." Shuttleworth wiped his red nose with a damp, shredded tissue, bits of which fell to the floor like April snow. "Don't get too close. I still don't feel well."

"You look terrible, Byron. Why aren't you home in bed?"

"Go across the room so that I can close the door for a minute. I don't want you catching what I've got."

Grant was momentarily troubled by the dean's somewhat suspicious behavior, but then it dawned on him. He had applied for a ten-thousand-dollar summer stipend to fund research for his upcoming novel, and the request must have been approved. Shuttleworth was no doubt here to deliver the good news personally.

Not wishing to spoil Shuttleworth's surprise, he resisted the powerful urge to smile, but he was overjoyed at the prospect of having an extra ten grand in his pocket. He would probably conduct his research at the Jersey Shore in an ocean-front rental with a large deck. What better place to craft the great American novel? Plentiful sunshine filling each day, seagulls wheeling noisily overhead, and the hypnotic sound of waves lulling him to sleep each night.

Shuttleworth cleared his throat and delivered the message in funereal tones.

"President Farnsworth got the facts a bit wrong at yesterday's faculty meeting. As it turns out, all eligible faculty members *except one* were granted tenure this year. I'm afraid you're that one, Grant."

Grant sank slowly and quietly into his chair. The voice deep inside his brain that urged him to kill someone was drowned out by the sound of dreams crashing to earth one by one all around him. What hurt most in that moment was the awful awareness that this miserable office he had longed to leave was probably far better than what awaited him out there.

Out there where? Would any self-respecting college hire an assistant professor his age? Unlikely. The junior slots went to people in their thirties. People with futures. Not rejects like him.

"How could that possibly happen?" Grant asked when the last of his dreams, a home of his own, finally landed with a dull thud. "How could Farnsworth have screwed up something so important? Is he a complete imbecile?"

If only you knew. "He simply misunderstood my message, and he feels terrible about it."

"So terrible that he sent you to set the record straight? Please be serious, Byron. But forget about that. How are you going to make this right?"

Shuttleworth shook his head despondently. "There's no way to make it right, Grant. The tenure committee has the final say, and its decision was clear. Farnsworth just got the facts wrong, so he said what he said yesterday."

Grant paused to imagine what the rest of his day would be like. People who had heard yesterday's good news would walk up and congratulate him, and he would be forced to tell the sad story again and again. Then, as the word gradually spread across campus, he would find people avoiding him, rushing off in the other direction rather than embarrass him further. What could they possibly say to someone who had been publicly humiliated in such spectacular fashion?

"So that's that?" Grant thundered. "I'm supposed to accept being turned into the campus laughingstock because Farnsworth had his head up his butt?"

"I'm here to apologize, Grant," the dean said feebly, a tissue at his nose, "and there's nothing more I can do."

"Have you bothered to ask Hannah Grackle what she thinks about this?"

"I didn't speak with her directly," Shuttleworth admitted, "but, yes, I know exactly where she stands. She made her position completely clear."

"And the opinion of my department chairperson doesn't matter to you?"

The dean's eyes narrowed as the confused look spread across his face. He felt he had gotten lost somewhere along the way.

"I'm not following you, Grant. When Hannah heard the announcement yesterday, she went to my office and demanded an immediate correction."

It was Grant's turn to look confused. "Wait, she told me she was one hundred percent behind me on tenure. Why would she . . ."

Shuttleworth quickly interrupted.

"Grant, I've heard through the grapevine that the committee would have voted yes had it not been for Hannah's demand that you be denied tenure. The committee would never consider overriding the wishes of the applicant's department chairperson."

"She swore she was on my side," Grant murmured.

"She wasn't." Shuttleworth paused for a moment. "I'm terribly sorry about this, but all I can do is send an email to the entire faculty explaining the mistake."

Grant grabbed the handouts for his 8:00 a.m. class and walked out of the office wordlessly. He had the entire day ahead of him, and he was reasonably sure every single minute of it would be excruciating.

11.

Distracted by thoughts of his impending doom, Grant was only partially present for his first class of the day, there yet not there. In fact, the session was a complete blur except for the lavender tank top being worn braless by Rachel Behr, the shapely and shamelessly flirtatious junior who always sat in the first row. As usual, she and her sixteen fellow slackers had not bothered to read the assigned homework, but at least they had come to class. As long as they continued to do so, he would give them all courtesy C's for the semester. All, that is, except Rachel, who would be getting a well-deserved B on the basis of her considerable nonacademic attributes.

Grant ended the class after fifty minutes of shared boredom and waited at the front of the room as his students filed out.

"Have a great day, Professor Hunter," Rachel said cheerfully. As she stood, her tight lavender top grew momentarily tighter, and she smiled when she noticed that he had noticed.

He sensed her B rising to an A.

Since his next class wasn't until 11:00, he decided to hit the gym for one of the last few times. Once the semester ended and he was stripped of his faculty credentials, he would no longer be able to enjoy the simple pleasure of shooting baskets on Hickston's new hundred-thousand-dollar maple court.

During his earliest days as a faculty member, Grant had played on the old court, a creaky, downtrodden expanse of what had appeared to be weathered barnwood. The flooring buckled in warm weather, developed gaping cracks during the coldest months, and had a long history of maiming players with splinters the size of bamboo skewers.

Those days were gone, of course. The cost of the new court had been covered several times over by the athletic department revenue derived from back-to-back national championships. Thanks to Tex Brawner and his star Winston Churchill Mbongo, playing basketball on the Vultures' home floor was no longer a life-threatening experience.

Grant walked into the gym where his friend Jim McArdle was in the process of being destroyed in a game of one-on-one by Ty Chambers, the basketball team's starting point guard, who would soon be moving on to the NBA. Ty was taking it easy on the math professor, shooting only with his left hand and even then only from twenty feet or more, but the score was still 14-3 in Ty's favor. The final affront was a hook shot Ty launched from near the half-court line. The ball traveled forty-three feet in a high rainbow arc, hit the dead center of the shooter's square on the backboard, and ripped through the net with a crisp snapping sound.

"Another game, Professor McArdle?" Ty asked politely.

"Not unless you agree to play blindfolded."

Ty shrugged. "I guess I could try."

"I was just kidding, Ty. You'd still beat me anyway. Besides, I think Professor Hunter wants a shot at you," Jim cackled.

Grant shook his head. "I may look stupid, Ty, but I'm smart enough not to go one-on-one with a future NBA all-star."

Ty laughed and began draining three-pointers as Jim walked off the court wet, rumpled, and tired.

"That was a humbling experience," Jim allowed. "Remind me not to go up against Ty again."

"Don't go up against Ty again."

"Thanks, wise guy. So how's our newest tenured faculty member feeling on this fine morning?"

Grant looked up at the rafters, took a deep breath, and then spoke the words he knew he would be repeating all day long.

"Shuttleworth came to see me this morning," he said disconsolately. "He told me Farnsworth got the message wrong at yesterday's faculty meeting. All eligible candidates *except one* were granted tenure. I'm sure you can guess who the *one* was."

"Please tell me you're making a bad joke."

"It's no joke. I didn't get tenure. The committee chose not to over-rule Grackle."

"The one who claimed she was on your side."

39

"Right, that's the one."

Jim thought for a moment. "Since the president made the announcement publicly, isn't there any way you can hold him to it? Maybe you can argue it was a valid verbal contract."

"I'm not a lawyer, thank God," Grant said, "but I'm sure I can't sue anyone for making a mistake no matter how embarrassing it was for me. What Farnsworth did was stupendously careless, but it wasn't deliberate. I certainly have the right to appeal the decision, but no one on the committee is going to risk a war with Grackle on my behalf."

"You know, I didn't think it was possible for me to dislike Grackle more today than I did yesterday, but I was wrong. Students hate her, and so do almost all her colleagues. She's the one who should be leaving, not you."

Grant shrugged. "There's nothing I can do now except humiliate you in some one-on-one."

Jim shot him a look of friendly contempt.

"I'm ready, but make sure you don't expect any mercy from me. If you think you feel bad now," he taunted, "wait until I'm finished with you."

Grant went to the locker room and changed into his gym gear, then spent forty intense minutes battling his friend for the day's basketball bragging rights. After splitting the first four fifteen-point games, they battled for nearly twenty minutes in the championship game. Grant claimed the crown 27-25, winning by the mandatory two-point margin.

"Go on, Jim. You can say it. I was brilliant in that last game."

"I was actually wondering how one person could make so many lucky shots in a single game."

"Uh, please," Grant teased, "never use the word *lucky* around me. Remember who you're talking to."

"You're right. Sorry. Want to grab an early lunch?"

"I can't. I teach at 11:00."

"Then you are, indeed, a lucky man. I saw the menu online, and they're serving pot brush stew again."

"In that case, eat enough bristles for two. I think I'll just get a candy bar." After a brief pause he added, "In a few more weeks I may not be able to afford even candy bars."

Jim laughed good naturedly because he didn't know his friend was serious.

Grant was about to join the ranks of the miserably unemployed, and his checking account was nearly in the red.

12.

Grant endured the 11:00 a.m. class the same way a death row inmate awaits a last-second pardon, with every minute seeming like an hour.

Without Rachel Behr and her lavender tank top to distract him, he wallowed in self-pity the entire time while his students labored over a five-hundred-word essay on Robert Frost's poem "Mending Wall," which no one had bothered to read. Uppermost in his mind were the bills that would be coming due after he had received his final Hickston paycheck. He ultimately concluded he might have enough money for food if he gave up his apartment and lived in his twelve-year-old Kia Optima. But even then he would be destitute by September if he failed to land a new position.

His college teaching experience and two English degrees were worth next to nothing in a job market that favored tech-friendly youngsters capable of typing faster with their thumbs than Grant could with all ten fingers. He was in his early forties, had never used any software other than Word, and still didn't know how to delete voice messages from his cell phone. Basically, he was an old-school man of letters adrift in a world that favored scientists, technicians, and robots.

After class he bought a Snickers bar from the vending machine in Caterwaul Hall, trudged up the stairs to his office, and pulled the door shut. At the center of his desk someone had placed a printed version of the email Shuttleworth had sent to all faculty members an hour earlier. The dean greatly regretted the previous day's "erroneous announcement," the message said, and he apologized for any inconvenience it had caused anyone.

Grant was infuriated by the word *anyone*. How could any person other than him have been "inconvenienced" by the monumental blunder?

Perhaps Shuttleworth had been thinking of Grackle when he wrote the message. She certainly must have been angry to think that someone had dared to approve Grant for tenure despite her opposition, but would that have "inconvenienced" her in any way? Hardly.

The only person who had been "inconvenienced" was Grant, of course, but Shuttleworth had not found the courage to say something as direct as, "I regret that our fine colleague Grant Hunter was humiliated in this fashion after six years of faithful service to Hickston College."

Three gentle taps on the door took his mind off Shuttleworth's memo, which he crumpled and tossed in the wastebasket. He opened the door and said hello to Miranda, who looked as defeated as he felt.

"I'm so sorry," she said softly.

He stepped aside so that she could enter, then closed the door.

"If someone had let me know before the faculty meeting that I had been turned down," he said, "I would have been disappointed, of course. But this is much worse, Miranda. To be told I had been granted tenure and then have the rug pulled out from under me is really hard to take."

She settled into the chair alongside his desk and waited for him to sit.

"It's cruel beyond comprehension, Grant. Did Farnsworth at least call to apologize?"

He laughed derisively. "Of course not. He sent Shuttleworth, who arrived here before my eight o'clock class looking as though he had just clawed his way out of a grave."

"Shuttleworth is an empty suit."

"Name one administrator who isn't. But at least he told me why I was turned down." Grant explained how Grackle had stabbed him in the back after claiming to support his tenure bid. "But you're not surprised, are you? You told me yesterday you didn't trust Grackle."

"She's a wretch who will end up destroying herself, but not until she's trashed more good people like you."

Miranda spent the next thirty minutes attempting to boost Grant's spirits and to help him focus on the future, which she assured him would be bright despite this current setback. Although he listened attentively to the message, he seemed not to notice the messenger. Both the way she looked and the way she looked at him signaled a level of interest that went beyond a desire to dispense sisterly good advice. But he was oblivious. All Grant could see at the moment was his life circling the drain.

She took out her cell phone and slid her chair next to his so that she could show him something. Her Yves Saint Laurent Black Opium perfume seemed to envelope him in a spring garden kissed gently by vanilla, and for half a heartbeat his mind almost drifted away from his sorry predicament.

"This was posted on the Hickston HR website this morning." She rested her shoulder against his upper arm as she handed him the phone. "This could be a good move for you."

It was a job posting for a public relations director whose primary duty would be writing upbeat stories about the college and peddling them to any newspaper that might be interested.

He looked as though he had swallowed a mouthful of vinegar.

"A college p.r. director? Why on earth would I consider that?"

"Two reasons. First, it's a job, something you won't have in another few weeks. Second, it would allow you to retain credit for the six years you've already put in at Hickston."

"But a p.r. director?" He sounded as though they were talking about a job mopping bathrooms at Yankee Stadium.

"It's a writing job, Grant, and you're a writer."

"I'm not *that* kind of writer. I have no desire to be a p.r. flack."

"You'd rather wait tables at Margot's Grill?"

The fight went out of him. Was it the thought of scrounging for tips at a Steinville restaurant, or was it the beautiful jade eyes that implored him to at least consider taking an administrative position?

"I guess there's no harm in interviewing for the job."

"No harm at all. And you would still be able to do your own writing at night and on weekends."

Her comment struck a chord. He usually wrote at night anyway, and he knew that a number of famous novelists, George Orwell among them, had been highly productive in the wee hours of the morning.

"The position description says the job reports to Arthur Sproull. Any idea who that is?" he asked.

Miranda nodded. "The vice president for development."

"What does he develop?"

"Nothing, Grant. He's a fundraiser. He courts old rich people and tries to get Hickston into their wills."

"Ah, okay. Like the forty-million-dollar bequest Farnsworth announced yesterday."

"Exactly."

"And if I became Hickston's p.r. director," he observed, "I suppose I would have to write wonderful things about some drooling octogenarian who had been sweet-talked out of his or her fortune. Sounds kind of slimy to me."

"That's because it's a slimy business. But on the bright side," she countered, "you would also be able to write as much as you want about Winston Churchill Mbongo."

Miranda had done her homework. Grant loved basketball nearly as much as he loved writing, and the thought of writing about Winston pushed him over the edge.

He glanced at his watch. "Maybe I'll swing by Sproull's office before my next class."

"I think that's an excellent idea."

A man who takes a woman's direction, she told herself as she left his office, *is a man with unlimited potential.*

She was immensely pleased with Grant's progress. The more she saw of him, the more upside he seemed to have.

13.

Sproull's office occupied the entire second floor of Bluff House, a colonial home that at various times in the school's history had been a women's dormitory, a fraternity house, an infirmary, and an art gallery. Upon becoming Hickston's vice president for development, Sproull had made a compelling case for investing heavily in a space that would appeal to wealthy donors.

"Money begets money," he had told the president, "and major donors won't be tempted to invest unless they see evidence of a thriving enterprise. The moment they walk into my office, they need to feel they're in the company of someone who understands them."

The luxurious makeover had cost nearly a half million dollars, all of it siphoned from a generous 1963 gift intended to fund the establishment of a landscape architecture program. Sproull had argued at the time that no one would quibble over how the money was spent since the donor, Conrad Bluff, was long dead and had no living relatives.

"But aren't we required by law to honor the donor's wishes?" the president had asked.

"Not if we can't find the written agreement," Sproull had winked. "In this particular instance, the agreement was lost in a fire. These things happen."

The fire in question had been in the downstairs fireplace of Bluff House, but that was a detail neither Sproull nor the president planned to share with anyone.

The first thing Grant noticed when he entered Bluff House was the small plastic OUT TO LUNCH sign on the receptionist's desk in the foyer. It appeared, in fact, that everyone on the first floor was out to lunch. Then he saw the brass nameplate on the wall near the staircase:

46

ARTHUR G. SPROULL, VICE PRESIDENT. A clicking sound from upstairs caught his attention, and he began climbing the richly carpeted stairway to the inner sanctum.

Stepping onto the second floor of Bluff House was momentarily like entering the private wing of an art museum. Caravaggio, Rembrandt, Vermeer, Botticelli, and da Vinci were there along with a number of more contemporary masters. But a second glance revealed that all the images hanging on the beige walls were cheap reproductions purchased online for less than fifty dollars each. The frames were worth considerably more than the paper prints they contained.

Grant turned to his left when he heard the clicking sound again and saw Sproull with his back to the staircase. Putter in hand, the vice president was lining up another shot at the ball-return machine nestled in the thick off-white carpet that covered the entire second floor. A smooth stroke sent the ball fifteen feet to the dead center of the plastic ramp, and an electric plunger fired the ball back to him for another try.

When Grant knocked gently on the wall, Sproull stiffened like a shoplifter caught stuffing a T-bone steak under his shirt and slowly looked over his shoulder. He was relieved to see someone other than Porter Farnsworth standing there.

"Who are you?" he asked indignantly.

"Grant Hunter."

Sproull rested his putter against the wall and walked over.

"The name sounds familiar."

"Maybe you saw it in an email from Dean Shuttleworth this morning."

"Oh, right," Sproull said, plainly amused. "The English professor who was granted tenure for less than twenty-four hours. What a special sort of ass Byron can be when he puts his mind to it."

"Actually, it was Farnsworth who got the message wrong yesterday."

"Thanks to Shuttleworth. He's not fit to manage the grounds crew much less the faculty. So why are you here?"

"Uh, well, I saw the posting for a public relations director."

"And?"

"And I wanted to learn more."

"Why didn't you ask the receptionist downstairs? She has all the information."

"There's no one downstairs."

"Oh. In that case, there are three things I can tell you. First, the job pays sixty thousand dollars per year."

Grant forced himself not to smile. Since he was currently earning forty-six thousand, he could boost his earnings by thirty percent if he took the p.r. job. He was suddenly interested in a position that he still believed was beneath his dignity.

"Second," Sproull said, "the posting specified that we would not consider candidates who did not have college p.r. experience. Third, and most relevant, we already filled the position."

Grant thought he had misheard.

"How can the job already be filled if you only posted it this morning?"

"We knew we were going to promote the assistant director, but HR insisted we post the position anyway. That's how it usually happens. Besides," he quipped, "a man named Grant Hunter should be writing grant proposals, not press releases. *Grant hunter*, get it?"

Grant followed Sproull to the aircraft carrier of a desk that was berthed at the room's far end. The piece, ornately French and worth more than one hundred and fifty thousand dollars, stood before windows that provided inspiring views of the campus and the Hudson River. To the right of the desk and carefully placed at the edge of an eighteenth-century wool rug was a jaw-dropping Louis XV settee that throughout Sproull's reign had accommodated the privileged rumps of his wealthiest guests. The settee and two matching armchairs had cost the college a cool one hundred thousand dollars. Across from the sitting area was a stunning fruitwood conference table that had once been tended by servants in a modest French palace. The table and its ten carved chairs had set Hickston back another two hundred thousand.

"Okay, so do you have an opening for a proposal writer?" Grant asked innocently in response to Sproull's comment.

"No," Sproull said, nervously drumming his fingers on the desktop. "And if we did, we would naturally hire a person with extensive experience. In other words, not someone like you."

"Then maybe you should hire a golf pro to help you work on your putting. If you ripped out all this fancy carpeting and replaced it with artificial turf, I'm sure you could lower your handicap in a few months."

Sproull's face turned crimson. "How I spend my lunch hour is none of your business," he sputtered. "So just go pack your things since you'll be departing soon."

Grant left and hurried down the staircase, but he stopped when he reached the first floor and once again heard the clicking sound from upstairs. He crept quietly to the second floor, took his cell phone from his pocket, and snapped a photo of the vice president at his makeshift putting green.

Sproull heard the sound.

"Did you just take a picture?" he screamed. "I'm talking to you. Get back here!"

Grant bounded down the stairs without responding. He had no idea how he would end up using the photo, but he was confident the right moment would come along.

14.

During the final two and a half weeks of the semester, Grant suffered from what psychologists commonly refer to as approach-avoidance conflict. He desperately wanted the academic year to end so that he no longer had to endure the pity being heaped on him by his more fortunate colleagues. At the same time, however, he prayed for the semester to be extended by another month or two because he had lost hope of finding another job.

He applied to teach English at the local public high school but was turned down because he didn't have a state teaching certificate. A few days later, the local private school also said no, freely admitting it could hire someone half his age for half his salary. Three other potential employers, Steinville Taxi, McDonald's, and a debt collection call center, brushed him off because he was overqualified and would leave as soon as something better came along.

Miranda, slightly overwhelmed by her own end-of-semester workload, stopped by to see Grant when she could, each time wishing she could find a way to pull him out of his deepening funk. She still felt bad about his unpleasant experience with Sproull the Ghoul since she's the one who had prodded him to apply for the p.r. job, but he dismissed her concern out of hand. He really hadn't wanted that kind of job anyway, he assured her, and remained committed to writing for a living.

"I may starve in the process," he said half-jokingly, "but I won't be the first writer to have done so."

If he did starve, he would, in fact, join authors like Herman Melville, Edgar Allan Poe, Henry David Thoreau, and Emily Dickinson in dying penniless. But that was hardly his intention. He believed he had great novels hiding within him, and he was confident he could earn a good living by liberating them. He would never earn as much as someone like James Patterson, who had banked nearly a billion dollars by writing prolifically, but he was willing to settle for less since his goal was to produce literature, not what he termed "pop entertainment."

Despite the embarrassing end to his Hickston career, he gamely muddled through the customary year-end routine. He taught his final lessons to groups of listless undergraduates, graded research papers that might have been produced by monkeys, administered a series of final exams, and honored his posted office hours even though no students ever came to see him. This odd period of his life seemed even odder because of Steinville's erratic weather. One day the temperature would rise above eighty, and a few days later it would plummet and leave a dusting of snow in its wake.

On one particularly cold late-April morning, when the thermometer registered only twenty-three degrees, Hannah Grackle slipped on an icy patch in the faculty parking lot and fractured her right wrist. To Grant's immense disappointment, she lived to tell the tale. But he derived a great deal of satisfaction from the fact that she would likely be in howling pain for a while and then would suffer even more pain once the physical therapy sessions began. It had never been his style to delight in the misfortune of others, but for her he gladly made an exception.

Grant was alone at his desk one afternoon when someone from behind said, "I haven't seen you in the gym lately." He turned and was delighted to see Tex standing in the hallway. The coach wore a compassionate smile and held a plain white envelope in his left hand.

"I've been busy wrapping up loose ends," Grant replied. "Teaching, grading, trying to find a job. All the fun stuff."

Tex came in and sat down. "Any luck on the job front?"

"A few NBA teams would like me to play point guard for them, but I'm not sure I want to travel that much."

"I'm glad you haven't lost your sense of humor."

"Why do you think I'm kidding?"

"I've seen you play."

"Oh, right. Well, to answer your question, no, I have nothing going on the job front. Failed English professors are as much in demand as five-foot-two power forwards."

"You're not a failed English professor," Tex countered. "You're a fine professor who had the misfortune of coming into contact with Grackle. Something will turn up."

"Maybe you could hire me to mop up the basketball court when sweaty players drip all over it."

"I could, but the job doesn't pay. All you get is a meal pass on game days."

"Seriously? Those kids bust their butts like that for free?"

"Sure. But they get to see every home game, even the ones that are sold out, and they're able to watch from courtside. Plus, as I said, they each get a free meal."

"I might need free meals."

"I don't have any meal passes," Tex said with a grin, "but I do have this for you." He handed over the envelope.

Grant's eyes widened when he saw the two season passes.

"Hey, I wasn't serious about wanting free tickets."

"Fine, I'll give them to someone else," Tex said as he reached for the envelope.

"Not a chance! I may starve by the time you win your next NCAA championship, but I'll die happy. Thanks, friend. But why two season tickets?"

"That was Sherry's idea. She can't stand seeing a happy bachelor. So now you'll have to find someone to bring to the games."

Tex failed to mention that his wife, Hickston's former alumni director, was close friends with Miranda Davignon, who was about to develop a passion for college basketball. He would let Grant learn that for himself.

"It's probably the only date I'll be able to afford."

Tex turned serious. "I'll tell you what I always tell my players: you can't be a winner if all you think about is losing. I'm an excellent judge of talent, Grant, and I have complete faith in you."

"But not as an NBA point guard?"

"That's definitely not in the cards, but I know you'll be a star off the basketball court. Think like a winner. Let nothing and no one get in your way."

A firm handshake, and Tex was off to meet a seven-foot-two recruit from Senegal who already had NBA scouts salivating.

Grant carefully tucked the season tickets inside his badly scuffed leather briefcase and went back to grading papers. Oddly, though, for the first time in weeks he didn't feel like a loser.

15.

With two days remaining before the end of the academic year, Grant was running well ahead of schedule. He had already submitted grades for all but one of his classes and figured he should be able to wrap things up completely by early the next morning. Thanks in large part to Tex's encouraging words, he had reached an uneasy peace with his situation and was ready to tackle whatever came next.

Shortly before eleven a.m. he was at his desk scribbling remarks in the margin of a research paper when Juliet Swanson marched into his office without knocking. She had been seductively sweet during her first visit, when she had all but invited him to bed, but she now dropped all pretense of civility. She had gotten an A on the final exam, an achievement comparable to the conquering of Mount Everest by Sir Edmund Hillary, thereby raising her class average to a solid D. But in an act of immense generosity, Grant had given her a B for the semester. He was well aware that she didn't deserve it, but he was willing to reward her for the effort she had finally put forth. He hoped it might help motivate her to work harder for the remainder of her Hickston career.

"You said I'd get an A for the course if I aced the final, which I did," she snapped without preliminaries. Her hands were balled into tight fists, and her silver eyes flashed like lightning. "Then you gave me a B instead."

"Good morning, Miss Swanson," he said mildly. "Most students knock before barging into my office."

"I'm not most students, and there's nothing good about this morning. You gave me a B for the semester even though I got an A on the final exam, so you're going to change the grade."

Grant calmly removed a black appointment book from a pocket of his briefcase and turned to the date of Juliet's first visit.

"Here's the note I wrote to myself after you stopped by a few weeks ago. *Has an F so far. If she gets an A on the final, reads all novels, and attends all classes, consider a B for the semester.* That's what I told you, Miss Swanson, and you know it. The B you got for the course is without exception the greatest gift I've ever given anyone who had been running a solid F for an entire semester."

When the look she gave him didn't cause him to fall dead on the office floor, she issued her final warning.

"I know *exactly* what you said to me that day, and if you don't give me the A you promised, I'll go to your department head as soon as I leave here."

"Do you need directions?" he asked helpfully.

She gave him the finger before flying out of his office and racing down the hall in the direction of Grackle's office. *No good deed goes unpunished,* he reminded himself. He never should have told her she might be able to get a B for the course, and in the end he should have given her the D she deserved, even with an A on the final exam. But since his time at Hickston was nearly over, this tempest in a teapot didn't matter to him in the least.

Thankfully, Juliet Swanson was no longer his problem.

Or so he thought.

Thirty minutes later he received two visitors: Grackle, her face contorted with hate and her right forearm in a large plaster cast, and Byron Shuttleworth, his customary pale and cowardly self.

"You're going down for this, Hunter," Grackle thundered as she charged into his office.

Grant ignored her and smiled at the dean.

"Hello, Byron. Where'd you get the pet ape?"

Shuttleworth ignored the question while Grackle fumed. Her left eye began twitching uncontrollably.

"One of your students has told Professor Grackle that you demanded sex from her," Shuttleworth said.

"The thought of having sex with Hannah makes me nauseous."

"Not sex with Hannah," the dean clarified. "I meant sex with the student."

"He knows exactly what you mean, you imbecile," Grackle shouted. Then to Grant, "Offering a higher grade in return for sexual favors is a criminal offense."

"So is violating a verbal contract," Grant fired back. "You told me you would support my tenure application, then single-handedly made sure I was turned down."

"My word against yours," she said smugly.

"And it's my word against Juliet Swanson's. But I also happen to have supporting documentation for the conversation I had with that little tramp a few weeks ago."

Grant showed Shuttleworth the appointment book as well as a record of all the failing grades Juliet had logged during the semester. After reviewing the evidence and listening patiently to Grant's unvarnished account of Juliet's brazen sexual advances, Shuttleworth turned to Grackle.

"Obviously, she didn't deserve a C," he announced, "much less an A. And as far as her accusation goes, it seems to me a clear case of a student who's willing to say anything in order to get a grade she doesn't deserve."

"I believe her story one hundred percent," Grackle said bitterly, "so I'll change her grade to the A she deserves."

"In return for sexual favors?" Grant asked with a straight face. "A lot of us *have* been wondering about you, Hannah."

She yelped like a puppy whose tail had been stepped on, then spun and practically ran from the office. In her haste to leave, she caught the toe of her right shoe on the wooden door sill, stumbled clumsily into the hall, and snapped her left wrist when she hit the floor with a harsh thud.

Grant wordlessly locked his office door and left for lunch, leaving Shuttleworth to minister to Grackle, whose screams of pain echoed through all four floors of Caterwaul Hall. It would have been better if she had broken her neck, he thought, but it was a fortunate outcome nonetheless.

He took it as evidence that life, despite the long odds, is sometimes fair.

16.

Grant was walking toward Vulture Commons when Miranda called to him from behind, and he waited for her to catch up. Since she had finished teaching for the year, she was dressed more casually than usual in a white silk tie-waist top, tastefully clingy jeans, and expensive suede loafers. All morning long a number of colleagues, both male and female, had commented on how attractive she looked, but Grant seemed not to notice either her summery outfit or her glowing smile. He had food on his mind.

"Are you on your way to eat?" she asked.

"I'm going to the dining hall. Whether I actually eat there depends upon whether anything on the menu sounds nonlethal."

"I had beef stew there a couple of weeks ago, and I think I found . . ."

"Brush bristles."

"Yes, exactly. Do you think that's what they were?"

"I'm positive. Jim McArdle ate one of them and lived. So I assume they're either nonpoisonous or extremely slow-acting."

She scrunched up her face and said, "Maybe we should drive to town instead."

"I can't. I have to finish grading a few papers and exams."

"How's everything going?"

He grinned. "The grading is going fine, but you won't believe what just happened."

As they strolled toward the dining hall, he merrily recounted the visit by Grackle and Shuttleworth. Miranda wasn't amused. She was horrified by Juliet Swanson's accusation, but she reserved the greater part of her wrath for Grackle, who had considered Grant guilty until proven innocent.

"Too bad she didn't break more than her wrist," she said after hearing the full story.

"I was thinking the same thing, actually, but in another forty-eight hours Grackle will no longer matter to me. I'll be off writing somewhere, and she'll be Hickston's problem."

They stopped inside the Vulture Commons lobby to check the day's menu, which offered two choices: a grilled ham-and-cheese sandwich with a side of potato chips and hearty beef stew. Some clever student had used a permanent marker to change *hearty beef stew* to *heart-stopping bristle stew.*

"Do you think it's still the same stew from a few weeks ago?" Miranda asked cautiously.

"Probably. I suspect they've been having trouble getting rid of it."

"Then I suppose I'll get the grilled sandwich. Surely they can't ruin something as simple as that."

"They'll undoubtedly do their best." He looked from the top of the stairway to the dining area below. "But I don't see any bodies on the floor, so we're probably okay."

They went downstairs, grabbed their greasy plastic trays, and shuffled along the serving line together. Grant got the grilled ham-and-cheese sandwich but said no to the potato chips. Miranda, mistaking Vulture Commons for a restaurant, said she wanted to substitute a small salad for the chips. The old man behind the counter could not have been more perplexed if he had been asked to recite the Declaration of Independence in Chinese. After looking around helplessly for the missing supervisor, he finally asked the even older woman next to him for advice. She briefly stopped ladling congealed stew into a bowl that had a jagged chip on its rim.

"We're not allowed to substitute," she screeched toward the hearing aid in his right ear. The sudden exertion of speaking triggered an unpleasant respiratory reaction, and she sneezed several times over the steam table before going back to ladling stew for the student who had just walked out in disgust.

"We're not allowed to substitute," the old man dutifully repeated for Miranda even though she and everyone else in the dining hall had heard his colleague. "Do you want the chips?"

Unwilling to argue the point, she agreed to take the chips. He swiped his bare hand across the front of his soiled apron, grabbed a large handful, and dropped them on the plate. As she left the serving line, Miranda dumped the chips into a trash bin that some considerate employee had placed there.

She followed Grant to a small table in the room's farthest corner, where he took a large bite of his sandwich, pronounced it dry but edible, and continued eating. Miranda forced down half her sandwich, then turned to the topic of Grant's impending unemployment.

"You seem to be taking your situation better today than you had been," she said earnestly. "I'm glad."

He paused to wash down the last bit of charred crust with a sip of water, then told her about the visit from Tex.

"What did he say?"

"Basically, he told me to focus on what I want and then go get it."

"Sounds reasonable to me."

"And to me as well. Do you know how many English department jobs are available in American colleges and universities right now?"

"No idea."

"Thirty-three, according to the *Chronicle of Higher Education*, which I spent nearly two hours reading last night. Thirty-three jobs, thirty-one of them requiring a Ph.D., and there are probably a hundred candidates for every position. So why should I kill myself trying to get a job I don't even want, Miranda? I want to be a writer, not an English professor."

"Then you should write. But . . ."

"But?"

A long pause followed. "I should probably mind my own business."

"No, tell me what you're thinking."

She took a deep breath. "Well, I'm thinking that there's only a tiny and shrinking market for what I guess you'd call *literary fiction.* If you write serious literature, you'll run the risk of starving."

"I guess I've always assumed that most writers pretty much starve."

She tilted her head slightly and gave him a curious look.

"You're kidding, right?"

"Kidding about what?"

"That most writers starve. I guess you've been so focused on writing the great American novel that you haven't done any market research."

"Okay, I know James Patterson is rich, but he's probably the exception to the rule."

"Not true. In fact, the people who make the most money write romances, which generate about two billion dollars a year in sales."

He was dumbfounded. "Romances as in love stories?"

"Correct. Readers can't get enough of them. So if you're looking to support yourself as a writer, you should consider writing what buyers want to read. I love literary fiction," she emphasized, "same as you, but I certainly wouldn't be willing to starve while writing it."

"What kind of money do romance writers make?"

"It depends on how good you are, but I know Nora Roberts is worth about four hundred million dollars."

"Four hundred *million?*"

"Yes. It appears that the genre has a stable core of about thirty million readers, nearly ninety percent of them women. So do the math, Grant. If you write something that attracts even ten percent of that market," Miranda said, "you're a millionaire."

The word *millionaire* resonated with Grant. However much he wanted to write the great American novel, he couldn't turn his nose up at the idea of becoming rich by sitting at a laptop banging out romances for a few hours each day. He had grown up in a happy home, but it had become clear to him at a tender age that his parents, Matt and Tammy, were constantly on the brink of financial ruin. Matt had managed a small-town hardware store for more than twenty years until Home Depot showed up and promptly put the store out of business. He then swallowed his pride and took a job supervising Home Depot's paint department for two-thirds of his old salary. Tammy, meanwhile, had been a part-timer in a travel agency until Americans stopped using travel agencies and began making their own reservations over the internet. After that she had worked part-time as a receptionist for a local law firm.

Given the family's precarious financial situation, Christmas for the Hunter kids had always been a casino. Sometimes they hit the jackpot, and sometimes they came away empty handed. Grant would never forget the Christmas of his ninth year, when he and his older sister were given bright-red envelopes containing IOUs. For the next two weeks he told his friends about all the imaginary gifts he had received, including the white pony that was being kept for him at an uncle's ranch.

Reminded of those old wounds, Grant suddenly realized he was on the same path his parents had followed all their lives: small jobs with little pay and absolutely no security. So he had a choice to make. He could scratch out a meager existence writing serious literature, or he could grab the brass ring.

The brass ring won. If Nora Roberts could earn four hundred million dollars by writing romances, he could too.

You can't be a winner if all you think about is losing, Tex had said. And he was right. It was time to think about winning.

17.

"I still have one major logistical problem," Grant noted as he and Miranda left Vulture Commons.

"What's that?"

"I need food and a roof over my head while I write, and so far I've been turned down for every job I've considered. Did I tell you I applied to be a cashier at Walmart yesterday and was rejected?"

She laughed until she realized he wasn't kidding.

"You're serious?"

He nodded. "The kid who interviewed me said I was overqualified and would leave as soon as something better came along. Which is true, of course. But still, to be rejected by Walmart stings."

Miranda stopped at a bench amid an expanse of golden daffodils that had been planted among the shade trees decades earlier. She sat, patted the place next to her, and waited for Grant. He glanced nervously at his watch.

"I know you have work to do," she said patiently, "but this will take only a minute. I may have a solution for your logistical problem."

Once he was seated, she told him that her friend Naomi Perlmutter, an associate professor of archaeology, was preparing to leave on a six-month sabbatical to Israel, where she would be digging for artifacts in the Negev Desert. Before she left, however, Naomi needed to find a trustworthy live-in sitter for her Steinville home.

"She's willing to pay fifty dollars a day, which is more than enough for food and gas. You'd have a comfortable home in a lovely neighborhood and could write all day long."

Grant did the math and said, "That's nearly nine thousand dollars over six months. And I don't have to pay any of her bills?"

"No, she pays all the bills. All you have to do is live there and watch over things."

"What kinds of things?"

"Water the plants, mow the lawn once a week, take in her mail, and call her in the event of an emergency. Oh, and feed the cat," she added casually.

"It sounded great until you got to the cat part," he said with a pained expression. "I'm not sure I could do it."

"You never had a pet cat?"

"I had a pet turtle for a few months. I wanted a dog, but my parents wouldn't let me have one. As for cats, well, I've always been sort of afraid of them."

Miranda failed to hide her surprise.

"I've never met anyone who's afraid of cats. Dogs, yes. But cats, no. What is it about cats that bothers you?"

"They're stealth predators, Miranda. Lions, tigers, panthers, house cats—there's no difference except for the size."

"And except for the fact that no one has ever been killed and eaten by a house cat. They might scratch or bite if mistreated," she told him, "but I can't picture you mistreating an animal."

"I don't think I've ever mistreated anyone or anything," he said with obvious sincerity, "but I still don't trust cats."

"Tell you what. Take the house-sitting job, and I'll come over and coach you on feeding the cat and cleaning the litter box."

"Whoa, wait a second. That's the first mention of a litter box."

"It's a *house* cat, Grant, meaning it doesn't go outside. So there's a litter box involved."

"I've never cleaned a litter box."

"Of course you haven't," she said calmly, "and, as I just said, I'll come over and teach you how."

"You're sure?"

"I promise."

Grant took his time weighing his options. He could starve in a cardboard hut in some Steinville alley, or he could live in a comfortable home with a cat. The cardboard hut had a slight edge until Miranda placed her hand on his forearm and looked him in the eyes.

"I'll help you take care of the cat," she vowed, "and you can make me a hamburger on the grill now and then. How's that?"

"She has a grill?"

"A gigantic Weber grill, yes."

"I don't think I've ever met Naomi," he said.

"Then we'll go to her house later today when you're finished grading. Okay?"

He nodded. "I'll call you when I'm finished."

"I'll be waiting."

They left campus at 4:00 in Miranda's black BMW X5. Like the two million dollars in her bank account, the vehicle had been part of the divorce settlement. In 2021 her ex-husband, a successful stockbroker in midtown Manhattan, had placed a huge bet on an inconsequential tech company few people had ever heard of. His after-tax profit of four million dollars had been split two ways when Miranda divorced him over his torrid affair with a twenty-year-old hairstylist.

"Thanks for driving," Grant said as she exited the faculty lot and turned onto Hickston Road. "My car's a mess."

She had seen his car, an eleven-year-old Hyundai Sonata with nearly two hundred thousand miles on it. The exterior was in dismal shape thanks to a bad hail storm in 2018 and long exposure to acid rain. But the interior was worse, an untidy cross between a locker room and a library. The back seat held not one but two basketballs, a dented ski helmet, a slightly moldy softball glove, and boxes filled with books from all the classes he had taught since receiving his master's degree. The rear floor was littered with used napkins and greasy bags from fast-food restaurants as well as an odorous pizza box containing a petrified mushroom slice.

"I'm sort of a neat freak," she noted. "I bring my car in once a week to have it washed."

"I stopped washing mine when it passed one hundred thousand miles. Now it's basically a second home. Whatever doesn't fit in my apartment goes into the Hyundai."

"When your books start selling," she said encouragingly, "you'll be able to buy any car you want, and your home will be large enough to store everything. I have complete faith in you."

He turned and looked at her.

"You're the second person to say that this week."

"Really?" A warning flag went up. "Who's the other?"

"Tex."

She relaxed again. "I guess Tex and I see something in you that you don't."

"And what might that be?"

"Genuine writing talent, of course, but also honesty. That's a winning combination." She paused for a moment. "I also like that you're not full of yourself, which most people are. You don't spend your time trying to be important, and that's rare in academia."

"My parents taught me to live and let live. They never believed that someone else's success cost them anything, if you know what I mean."

"I do. I was married to a man who believed that life is a zero-sum game. If someone else won, he felt that he had lost. It's an absolutely horrible way to live, Grant, and I hope you never change."

He laughed. "If I haven't changed by now, I think I'm safe."

Miranda drove a mile and a half along Hickston Road before turning onto Featherly Way, Steinville's most coveted address. Unlike the modest, boxy dwellings they had seen since leaving campus, the homes on Featherly Way were mostly imposing, immaculately maintained structures occupied by the town's wealthiest residents. The smallest lot was one acre, the largest five. One home in particular caught Grant's eye. It had a long paver driveway leading to the front steps, and both sides of the driveway were lined with mature cherry trees that showcased a dazzling display of pink blossoms.

"Wow, now that's my kind of house," he said.

"My kind as well," she replied coyly. "Actually, it *is* my house. Naomi lives just down the road."

"Wait a second. That's your house?" She nodded. "How does a French professor manage to afford a big BMW and a house like that?"

"My ex wanted the home in Aspen, and I wanted this. I never liked Aspen anyway. Way too pretentious for my taste."

"Any other surprises? Maybe a nice pied-à-terre in Paris?"

"Sorry, no. This home is already much more than one person needs," she told him, "so I certainly don't need a place in France."

"And Naomi lives down the street. What's her story?"

"She's fifty-four, single, and rich."

"Another wealthy ex?"

Miranda shook her head. "No wealthy ex and no rich parents. Eight years ago she won thirty million dollars playing Powerball for the first and last time."

"And yet she still teaches?"

"What can I tell you? She loves archaeology and teaching. If it weren't for the money, she might actually fall in love and get married. But she's afraid any guy who asks her to marry him will only be after her bank account."

"Isn't that why God invented prenuptial agreements?"

"It absolutely is," Miranda agreed, "but she thinks it's tacky for two people in love to have a contract that implies a failed marriage. So she plays the field, travels a lot, and keeps the money safe."

Naomi's home was lovely though not nearly as large as Miranda's. It was a classic brick ranch set well back from the road on a heavily wooded four-acre lot. Winding its way through the trees was a stone wall dating to the late eighteenth century, clear evidence of Steinville's colonial heritage. The entire front of the house was ablaze with bright-red rhododendrons that had been blooming there for the past thirty years.

Miranda pulled into the long driveway while Grant eyeballed the vast lawn that stretched from the roadway to the front sidewalk and then continued well beyond both sides of the house. He wondered how many hours a week he would need to devote to mowing that much grass, and Miranda seemed to read his mind.

"Naomi has a big riding mower," she volunteered as she parked in front of the two-car garage, "and she told me the job takes her a little less than an hour."

"I'm surprised she doesn't just hire someone. She can easily afford it."

"She likes to keep busy, especially outdoors. I have no idea how many hours she spends each day in her woods searching for Native American and Revolutionary War artifacts."

"Right here on her own property?"

"Uh, huh. She keeps some things for herself, but she also donates objects to the New York State Museum in Albany and to the Museum of the American Revolution in Philadelphia."

"And now she's off to hunt for more artifacts in a desert."

"As I said, she likes to stay busy."

Precisely how busy Naomi liked to stay became obvious when she opened the front door to greet them. Her foyer was a thriving jungle that featured dozens of her favorite plants, some of them touching the ceiling. Norfolk Island pines, birds of paradise, dragon trees, and towering parlor palms occupied huge ceramic planters, in front of which were low metal plant stands laden with African violets, begonias, gardenias, gloxinia, Christmas cacti, cyclamens, and orchids.

The hand she extended to Grant was strong and calloused, evidence of decades spent digging, scraping, and chiseling for history. She was a thin, extremely fit woman with long black hair, intense dark eyes, and an inviting smile.

"It's nice to meet you, Grant. I've seen you on campus," she said cheerfully, "but our paths never crossed. Miranda tells me you're a novelist."

He gave her an embarrassed smile. "She omitted the word *aspiring*. I've published a collection of short stories, but the next novel I write will be the first."

"And I can't wait to read it. Let me show you around the house."

The tour began in the living room, where the main attraction was the banquette alongside a wide and exceedingly sunny bay window. Instead of seat cushions, however, the entire bench was covered with large flower pots, each containing a different variety of hibiscus, all in full bloom.

"You certainly like plants," Grant managed to say without sounding discouraged. He pictured himself spending all day every day watering and misting Naomi's indoor flower farm.

"I *love* plants. They have a way of brightening even the darkest day. But wait until you see the kitchen!"

He couldn't wait.

The kitchen was at a back corner of the house and had two oversized multi-shelved greenhouse windows filled with small plants. Grant counted thirty flower pots before Naomi told him to look out the window at the largest rose bed he had ever seen. The perfectly round bed was thirty feet across and glowing with riotous color.

"Looks to me as though you have every type of rose on the planet," Grant observed.

"Not even close. I have only about a dozen of the one hundred and fifty species available, but I'm slowly getting there. They require a great deal of work, as you can imagine."

Yes, he could imagine.

"One more collection," Naomi announced as she led Grant and Miranda to the master bedroom. Roughly the size of Grant's entire apartment, the bedroom had a king bed at one end, a gas fireplace at the other, and a side wall that was essentially all glass from floor to ceiling. Running the entire length of the wall was a deep wooden planter that was home to a dozen birches, all of them seven feet tall. Sunlight streamed onto the upper branches from three large skylights that helped create a magical woodland feeling.

Grant was momentarily speechless.

"Are those real birch trees?" he asked.

Naomi nodded. "Silver birch. Aren't they wonderful?"

"They are, but I had no idea you could grow them indoors."

"With enough care, anything will grow indoors. The birches are fairly high maintenance," she observed, "but they're doing well so far."

The words *so far* rattled him. Was it merely an innocent turn of phrase, or did Naomi foresee the death and destruction a bachelor could visit upon all her beloved leafy friends? A stray thought crept into his mind: if he ended up killing all the greenery, would he be held liable in a court of law?

"Ready to look outside?" Naomi asked.

Noting Grant's blank stare, Miranda put her hand on his lower back and gave him a gentle shove in the right direction.

It was clear to her she was about to spend the next six months as a part-time gardener.

Her plan was coming together nicely.

18.

The outdoor tour of Naomi's home began with the front lawn, every blade of which was emerald green and free of bothersome insects. Notably absent were dandelions, crabgrass, chickweed, quackgrass, and the hundreds of other weeds that typically invade even the most pampered turf. Grant correctly assumed that the grass he now walked on was the product of endless backbreaking labor.

"This may be the most perfect lawn in America," he said, more to himself than to the women.

Naomi smiled like a proud parent. "It's simply a matter of using the right fertilizer, insecticide, and weed killer at the right time," she said offhandedly. "And lime, of course. I also go over the entire lawn once or twice a week with a dandelion weeder just in case there's an invader."

"What's a dandelion weeder?" he asked.

The question caught her off guard. She had assumed everyone over the age of eight knew what a dandelion weeder was.

"It's a hand tool, sort of like a long two-pronged fork. You have to dig nice and deep alongside the dandelion so that you can pull out the entire root. If you leave any root," she warned, "the weed grows right back."

She moved on to the wall of flawless rhododendrons that traveled the full length of the house. The shrubs were heavy with blooms the size of softballs, the result of precisely timed applications of liquid fertilizer throughout the growing season.

"They'll be blooming for another few weeks," she pointed out. "To help produce new buds, you have to cut off each flower once it fades."

He managed a feeble, "Sure." By his rough estimate, a thousand blooms would need to be removed. He was afraid to ask how many days that particular job would take.

They followed the same routine as they slowly worked their way around the entire house, stopping frequently for Naomi's running commentary on forsythias, black-eyed Susans, hostas, tulips, lilacs, hydrangeas, periwinkles, and all the other flowers and shrubs that thrived in full sun, full shade, or some delicate combination of the two. Grant was slightly delirious by the time Naomi announced that their final stop on the tour would be the garage. She punched in the code for the left door and gazed lovingly at her eight-thousand-dollar John Deere X580 lawn tractor with an engine that looked large enough to power a tank. The freshly polished machine occupied the center of a light-gray epoxy floor that was clean enough to eat from.

"This thing is a beast," she assured him, "and makes short work of the lawn. Have you ever used one?"

"I used a push mower when I was fifteen and nearly removed my right foot," he admitted, remembering the terrible argument his parents had gotten into following the incident. His mother had refused to let him touch the mower after that, much to his father's displeasure.

"Oh, this is much safer. It's basically like driving a car. But not quite as fast. You'll get the hang of it."

He wondered whether he would get the hang of it before or after mowing down all her prized shrubs. An encouraging smile from Miranda reminded him to think positive thoughts.

Grant looked over at the right side of the garage, where a silver Mercedes S 500 sparkled in reflected light. Naomi noticed his interest.

"That reminds me," she said. "The dealer told me it can't sit here unused for six months. Would you mind driving it now and then?"

"Uh, it looks kind of new, Naomi." He imagined himself peeling off the passenger side of her hundred-thousand-dollar Mercedes as he backed out of the garage.

"Not really. I've had it for about five months." That small detail taken care of, she said, "How about we go inside and talk over a glass of wine?"

"That sounds wonderful," Miranda answered.

They passed through the kitchen, picked up a chilled bottle of Cakebread Cellars chardonnay and a bowl of mixed nuts, then walked together toward the spacious screened porch at the back of the house.

Along the way Naomi kept looking around for something. When she finally stopped to peek behind the living room couch, Grant asked whether anything was wrong.

"No, I'm just wondering where Rajah is hiding. I'd like to introduce you to him."

She shrugged and walked into the sunroom.

"Rajah is Naomi's cat," Miranda informed him.

"He can be a little standoffish at first," Naomi added, "but he'll get friendly in a hurry once he realizes you're the person who'll be brushing him."

Grant turned to Miranda with fear in his eyes, but she simply nudged him toward the cushioned loveseat. Naomi sat across the coffee table from them, deftly uncorked the wine, and poured three generous servings.

"To artifacts in the Negev Desert!" Miranda said as they raised their glasses.

"And to Grant's novel," Naomi responded. "I hope you enjoy your stay here. Oops, there he is."

As Naomi hurried out of the room, Grant swallowed half his chardonnay in one gulp.

Miranda put her hand on his knee. "Are you okay?"

"I've never brushed a cat."

"There's nothing to it."

"I've also never driven a tractor."

"You'll be fine."

"And I'll never have a chance to write if I spend every day watering plants."

"I'm going to help you. Please don't worry, okay?"

"Introducing Rajah!" Naomi announced when she returned. She was holding what at first glance appeared to be a small leopard but was actually a large Bengal cat. Rajah weighed seventeen pounds, was as tall as a mid-sized dog, and was nearly two feet long, not counting his wildly twitching tail. He stared at Grant with piercing gold eyes and growled.

Grant nearly lost control of his bladder.

"He's a beautiful cat," Miranda opined.

"He is, isn't he? He's not quite full grown yet, but he's getting there."

71

Grant had suffered nightmares for several weeks after visiting a zoo at feeding time when he was in the fourth grade. He would never forget what those big cats had done to massive chunks of raw meat, and he still assumed that being eaten alive was the worst possible way to leave this world.

Naomi set Rajah on the floor, and he immediately jumped on the end of the loveseat, carefully stepped over Miranda's lap, and sat on his haunches staring into Grant's eyes. Grant forced a smile, but for the first time in his life he wondered whether predators can actually smell fear.

"I'll be right back," Naomi said.

As soon as she left the room, Grant turned his woeful eyes to Miranda and said, "I think it's getting ready to attack."

"Rajah's a *he*, not an *it*, and he likes you."

"How do you know?"

"Because you're still alive. Just kidding."

"Bad joke, Miranda."

"I'm sorry, Grant. But you're being silly. Rajah is a very sweet cat."

"Then why did he growl at me?"

"He's probably thinking about eating you," she giggled.

"Oh, that's really funny."

Naomi returned and handed Grant a large, soft bristle brush. As soon as he took it, Rajah climbed onto his lap, curled up, and waited.

"Whoever is holding the brush is his best friend," Naomi explained. "Just brush in one direction, from his head to his tail."

Grant did as he was told, and Rajah began to purr.

"He seems to like it," said Grant, happy to be alive.

"He loves it. Now, one last thing." She reached under the coffee table and retrieved a three-ring binder from the bottom shelf. "I've printed out simple instructions for how to take care of Rajah and the house. You can always text me if you have questions, but I think I've covered everything."

Since Grant was afraid to stop brushing Rajah, Miranda took the binder from Naomi and thumbed through all twenty-one pages while Grant looked over her shoulder. There were three pages for each day of the week, with the highly detailed instructions categorized by indoor chores, outdoor chores, and cat chores. The only thing missing, as far as Grant could tell, was time for him to eat, sleep, and use the bathroom. Sensing his discomfort, Miranda turned to him and said, "Piece of cake."

"It looks worse than it really is," Naomi offered between sips of wine. "Once you get into the routine, the indoor plants take about twenty minutes a day, and the outdoor plants require another twenty or so. Definitely less than an hour total."

Grant began to relax for the first time since arriving at Naomi's. An hour a day for the plants sounded entirely manageable, and he assumed that caring for Rajah would be even less time-consuming. Open a can of food twice a day and quickly run a brush over his fur now and then. Simple.

Naomi poured more wine for Grant, and he stopped brushing long enough to pick up his glass. Rajah looked up at him, slowly tested Grant's thigh with his front claws, and emitted a low moan.

"He's very spoiled," Naomi said. "He'd gladly stay there and let you brush him all day."

Grant forced a smile and took another gulp of chardonnay as the image of lions and tigers devouring chunks of raw meat came rushing back across the years.

He resumed the brushing, and the big cat settled down again, momentarily satisfied with his cozy situation.

19.

Grant gave his office a final once-over after clearing out the desk. The ancient dust remained undisturbed, and the mummified mouse under the bookcase promised to keep the secrets of yet another failed professor who had passed its way. After six years of capable and well-intentioned toil on Hickston's behalf, Grant was about to carry his academic career away in a cardboard box.

The semester had ended, he had submitted his students' grades, and his final check would be deposited in his dwindling bank account. There was nothing else to do but leave and try to forget.

The only person he saw as he walked down the hallway was old Georgette Mealey, who was talking on the phone as he passed. She waved, made a sad face, then resumed her conversation. Like most of his former colleagues, she hadn't said much to him lately, not out of malice but because she had no words that would help him. She considered him a wonderful person who had been treated shabbily, but she was powerless to do anything about it.

He attracted no attention as he hiked across campus with his heavy box. Most students had already departed for home, and those who remained were hurrying toward Vulture Commons, a sign that the day's lunch special was probably something other than bristle stew. Faculty members were also in short supply. Some would return in another week for the commencement ceremony while others had already left town to begin their summer vacations. As far as Grant knew, he was the only faculty member who had been shown the exit this year. Everyone else would return in September, ready to say and do the same things all over again with different faces staring at them.

Grant was passing the gym when Winston ran up to him and, without asking, snatched the cardboard box.

"You should not be carrying such a heavy box, Professor Hunter," he said sternly. "Whenever you need to carry something like this, call me, and I will help you."

"You're one of the world's finest people, Winston, but the box really isn't that heavy."

"Not for a young man like me, but . . ."

"Yes, I get your point. So what are you doing this summer?" Grant asked as they made their way to the faculty parking lot.

"I will be teaching a basketball camp in Cameroon. Two hundred students will be there! Can you imagine? Coach Brawner will join us for the final week, and maybe he will find future Hickston Vultures."

"I wish him luck, but he won't find another Winston Churchill Mbongo. You're a once-in-a-lifetime talent, and I can't wait to see all the things you accomplish in the future."

"And what about you, Professor Hunter? Do you have vacation plans?"

Grant hesitated, then said, "Actually, no. I didn't get tenure, so I'm leaving for good."

Storm clouds filled Winston's normally gentle eyes. "That is an outrage. You are one of the best professors in the entire world. How can they deny you tenure?"

"It's a long story, Winston, but basically it comes down to politics. Sometimes you can't overcome the efforts of the wrong enemy. But I'll be fine," he added. "I'll be writing full time."

"Then you will succeed as a writer, and I cannot wait to read your stories."

"And I can't wait to see you play again. In fact, I already have season tickets."

Winston gently set the cardboard box in the trunk of the battered Hyundai, then wrapped his gigantic arms around Grant.

"I wish you much success, Professor Hunter."

"Have a wonderful time in Cameroon, Winston. I'll see you again before long."

At exactly the same moment Grant was saying goodbye to Winston, Miranda was dropping Naomi off at Newark Liberty Airport and wishing her a rewarding stay in Israel. Naomi was on the 1:30 p.m. El Al flight to

Tel Aviv and would be staying for three nights at the glamorous Setai Hotel before beginning her work in the desert. She told Miranda she would be having dinner that night at one of Tel Aviv's finest restaurants with a handsome archaeology professor from Oxford.

"Will you be working with him the whole time you're in Israel?" Miranda asked.

"I plan to be doing a lot more than working with him," Naomi winked. "We met at a conference in London two years ago and spent more time in bed than we did discussing archaeology."

"But no long-term relationship?"

Naomi made a face. "Don't wish that on me. I'm too happy with my life. But what about you and Grant? He's a very appealing guy."

"He's also exceptionally slow to pick up on signals, if you know what I mean. I sometimes feel as though he won't get the message unless I parade naked in front of him."

"Then parade naked in front of him."

"I'd prefer something a bit more subtle."

"Subtlety takes time, Miranda, and time is our enemy. My advice: use these next six months wisely."

"I plan to."

Before Naomi and Miranda could haul the enormous suitcase from the back of the Beemer, a sharp-eyed skycap rushed over and took charge. Years of experience had taught him that passengers arriving in luxury vehicles were generally good for a ten-dollar tip, sometimes more, especially for international flights. Naomi handed him her first-class ticket, and he took care of the rest.

"Have a great time in Israel," Miranda said as she and Naomi shared a brief hug.

"And you have a great time with Grant."

"I'll certainly try."

Naomi remembered something as she turned to leave.

"Oh, by the way, my king bed vibrates," she said breezily. "The remote is in the top drawer of the night table."

By the time Miranda returned to Naomi's home, Grant had arrived and was nearly finished depositing his belongings inside the front door. Rajah had already curled up and fallen asleep in a box of clean T-shirts after sniffing through the new inventory.

"Interesting. You've decided to live in the foyer," Miranda said wryly.

"Actually, Naomi never told me where I should sleep. There are two guest bedrooms."

"Neither of which is for you. She expects you to sleep in the master bedroom."

Grant looked stricken. "But that's *her* bedroom."

"No, for the next six months it's yours. In fact, the entire house is yours for the next six months. That's the deal, Grant."

"You're sure about the bedroom?"

"I'm positive. Let me help you move some of this stuff."

"Uh, why don't you take the T-shirts?"

"You're still afraid of Rajah?"

"Suspicious, not afraid."

Miranda smiled, shook her head, and picked up the box. Rajah didn't move as she carried him to the master bedroom.

Once everything had been stashed in the appropriate closets and drawers, Miranda led Grant to the kitchen and pointed to an envelope that had been left on the island for him.

"When I picked Naomi up this morning, she asked me to make sure you read her note."

"Let me guess: it's an addendum to her twenty-one-page manual."

"I don't think so."

He opened the envelope and read the note thanking him for watching over her home and Rajah. The envelope also contained a two-hundred-dollar gift certificate for Les Bois, the best restaurant in Highland Falls.

"This is the place I was going to take you to after getting tenure," he said, obviously touched by Naomi's kindness. "Until I didn't get tenure, of course."

"But since you never disinvited me," she smiled, "I guess you still owe me a free meal. Oh, and Naomi left something else for you." She opened the door of the gleaming stainless-steel Viking refrigerator and pointed to a bottle of 2012 Dom Perignon champagne. "Naomi said it's okay to share it if you want to."

"Do you like champagne?"

"I love champagne, especially the kind that costs two hundred dollars a bottle. Naomi also made a quiche Lorraine last night, and it will take only a few minutes to heat." She studied his face hopefully. "If you're hungry, that is."

"I'm starving. If you heat the quiche, I'll open the champagne."

Miranda gave him a thumbs-up. "Sounds like a plan."

In fact, it seemed to her that the plan might actually be getting on schedule.

20.

Grant and Miranda ate lunch at a wrought iron table for two on the back patio. They agreed that Naomi's quiche was the best they had ever tasted, and the Dom Perignon was, as expected, exquisite. Brilliant sunshine, a mild breeze, and the exuberant song of a nearby house wren were fitting accompaniments to a perfect meal.

Over lunch she told him that in two days she would be leaving for an academic conference at Harvard, where she and several hundred other professors from around the country would share ideas on teaching foreign languages in the twenty-first century.

"It's an important topic," she noted, "because too many American students see no value at all in learning a foreign language. They seem to think it's up to everyone outside the U.S. to learn English."

"I wasn't aware this was an issue."

"It's a serious issue, actually. Enrollment in foreign language programs keeps dropping. At this rate, I may be waiting tables at a French restaurant one of these days."

"Not a chance, Miranda. I see you as a college president someday."

She rolled her eyes. "Please don't wish that on me. What an awful job that must be."

"Not if it's done right. And you'd be terrific. You're smart, personable, and decisive, and you've been helping turn Steinville around as a member of the town council. Everyone would love you."

"You're kind to say so, but I'm perfectly happy doing what I do." She paused for a sip. "And I know you're going to be happy writing now that you're finally doing what you're meant to do."

When they were finished eating, Grant got up to take the dishes inside, but Miranda suggested they first relax on the cushioned chaise lounges that sat side by side in the shade. That sounded wonderful to him, so they both got comfortable and quietly enjoyed the peaceful afternoon. The champagne worked its soothing magic on Grant, and he fell asleep almost immediately.

He woke with a start forty minutes later to find that the dishes had been cleared and the table wiped down. Miranda was kneeling on the rug inside the kitchen door brushing Rajah, who contentedly sniffed the fragrant spring air that passed through the screen.

"Welcome back," Miranda called to him.

"I'm really sorry, Miranda. I was going to take care of the dishes."

"But then the champagne put you down for the count," she laughed. "I fell asleep too. I just got up a few minutes ago."

"I don't usually have champagne for lunch." He considered what he had just said. "Actually, I've never had champagne for lunch."

"Then I'm glad you finally did. Want to say hello to Rajah?"

"What kind of mood is he in?"

"He's purring."

"That's pretty loud purring. Are you sure he's not growling?"

"Positive."

Grant took a deep breath and opened the door, then nearly got knocked over as Rajah bolted past him and sprinted into the backyard. The cat was racing up the trunk of a seventy-foot white pine before Miranda finished saying, "Dear God, you've got to be kidding me."

"Stay by the bottom of the tree in case he comes down," Grant yelled as he ran frantically through the kitchen toward the garage. "I'll get a stepladder."

Miranda looked at the massive tree, wondering what possible use a stepladder would be, as she composed an email in her head. *Dear Naomi, you haven't landed in Israel yet, but we've already lost your cat.* Then she glumly marched into the backyard, stood alongside the tree, and pleaded with Rajah to come down.

But Rajah was still on his way up. It was his first time in a tree, and he found the experience exhilarating.

Two minutes later Grant jogged into the yard with a six-foot step-ladder hoisted over his right shoulder. He quickly spread the ladder open, locked the braces, and began climbing.

"You're going up there?" Miranda shouted, her panic rising. Losing Rajah would be bad, but losing Grant would be worse.

"What choice do I have?"

Grant lifted himself from the ladder to the lowest branch and grabbed hold of the trunk.

"This is a bad idea, Grant."

"Do you want to call Naomi and tell her where the cat is?"

"No."

"Neither do I."

And with that he set out on the long journey, stepping confidently from one sturdy branch to the next. The branches were plentiful enough that he found climbing the pine even easier than climbing a ladder. But the higher he went, the thinner the branches became. He was fifty feet above the ground when the branch under his right foot snapped off cleanly and nearly sent him on his way down much faster than he had gone up.

Miranda called from below, but Grant couldn't tell what she was saying because he was focused on the cracking of the branch beneath his left foot. He hugged the trunk and cautiously lowered himself to a sturdier branch. As he pondered his next move, he looked down for the first time and grew slightly dizzy. Never a fan of heights, he now realized that climbing a tree after helping Miranda finish a bottle of Dom Perignon had not been a particularly wise move. Yet there he was, very much out on a limb, with Naomi's cat ten feet above him perched on a branch the width of a carrot.

Rajah stopped enjoying his first free-climb when he realized, as cats often do, that he had no idea to get down. Grant and Miranda would later read online that although climbing up is an instinctive behavior for cats, climbing down is a learned behavior—one that Rajah obviously had never been taught. After pawing at the tree trunk helplessly for a few minutes, he began meowing. In short order the meowing became loud enough for Miranda to hear it from the ground.

"What's wrong with him?" she shouted.

"He doesn't know how to get down."

Dear Naomi, Rajah fell from the top of your pine tree. I apologize profusely. "Should I call the fire department?"

81

"That only works in movies, Miranda. Firemen don't come out to rescue cats."

"Then what can we do?"

"I'm thinking."

Grant had two thoughts. One, climb back down and let Rajah fend for himself. Two, climb up higher and risk dying. Neither plan appealed to him.

"I have an idea!" Miranda called to him. "Show him the brush."

"I don't have the brush."

"I know." She waved the brush at him and then began climbing the ladder. By the time he realized what she had in mind, she was already on the first branch and on her way up.

"Stay there, Miranda. I'll come down and get it."

"No, I know how to climb a tree."

And, in fact, she did. She scrambled nimbly from branch to branch with the handle of the brush jammed into the back pocket of her jeans. She was making excellent progress when the gentle afternoon breeze became a moderate wind that rustled the pine needles and caused the upper third of the tree to sway from side to side. The higher she went, the more pronounced the motion became, and she froze. She wrapped both arms tightly around the trunk and announced that she couldn't go any farther.

"Stay where you are, and I'll come down and get the brush from you."

"Be careful," she said as a wind gust made the upper reaches of the old pine tree shudder. *Dear Naomi, Grant and I died trying to rescue Rajah.*

The minutes seemed like hours as Grant climbed down, pulled the brush from Miranda's back pocket, and then returned to his position ten feet below Rajah. He held the brush up, and the cat stopped howling.

"He sees the brush," Grant yelled to Miranda, who was returning to earth as quickly as she could.

"What's he doing?"

"Thinking, I guess."

Enticed by the thought of being brushed, Rajah decided it was time to walk headfirst down the tree. He put his two front paws on the trunk, shifted his weight forward, and immediately fell. Grant dropped the brush and prepared to catch a terrified Bengal cat, but miraculously Rajah managed to snag the trunk with his front claws when he was only two feet above Grant's head. The cat's body swung automatically into a more appropriate tail-down position, and all four paws clung to the tree with long, sharp claws.

Rajah gladly let go when Grant reached up and took hold of him. Cradled in Grant's left arm, he purred all the way down to the ground and was still purring when carried into the house and placed on the kitchen floor. He walked over to his bowl and began eating, apparently unfazed by his near-death experience.

His rescuers, on the other hand, looked like refugees from a war zone. Grant's T-shirt and jeans were coated with sap, and bloody scrapes covered his hands and arms. The back of Miranda's blouse had been torn down the middle when it snagged on a broken branch as she lowered herself from the tree, and it now resembled the battlefield flag of a defeated army.

"Well, that was an interesting end to a lovely lunch," Miranda said.

"At least no one died, right?"

"That's true. And who knows, maybe you'll build the episode into a novel one day."

He laughed nervously. "Maybe, but not anytime soon. At the moment, all I want to do is forget the whole thing ever happened."

She looked at her watch. "I'd better go home and change. The foreign language department's annual dinner is tonight."

"The English department never had one, at least as far as I know. Maybe Grackle just didn't tell me."

"No, Grackle isn't the type to host a party. A hanging, maybe, but not a party."

As she turned to leave, he said, "Would you like to have dinner tomorrow night at Les Bois?"

"I would love to have dinner tomorrow night at Les Bois," she said without hesitation. "As you might expect, French food is my favorite."

"How about if I get a seven o'clock reservation?"

"Perfect." Noticing that he seemed to have another question on his mind, she stepped closer and looked deep into his eyes. "Is there something else?" she asked sweetly.

"Uh, do you have time to show me how to take care of the litter box?" he asked tentatively.

Dear Naomi, I actually may have to parade naked in front of him before he gets the message.

"I cleaned it while you were sleeping," she said stoically, "so it's fine for today."

"Okay, thanks."

"You're welcome." She paused as an intriguing idea took shape. "If you want, I'll show you tomorrow night after dinner."

"That would be great."

Miranda went home hoping that for the first time in history a litter box might open the door to love.

21.

Grant began his full-time writing career in earnest by following Miranda's sage advice and doing some market research. He went online, paid six dollars for the first Amazon romance title that caught his fancy, and began reading the Kindle edition of *Ivy League Lust* by Marcy Yum.

Within the first twenty pages of the three-hundred-page novel, the two main characters, undergraduates Chet Hands and Fiona Feely, had sex seven times: three times in Chet's dorm room, twice under the football bleachers, once in a movie theater, and once on a rowboat in the middle of a lake. Then they got serious. By Grant's rough estimate, the author inserted a sex scene every page and a half throughout the remainder of the book.

Grant had seen a few torrid R-rated movies and had glanced now and then at online porn, but *Ivy League Lust* was an eye-opener in two key respects. First and foremost, of course, was the graphic, meticulously detailed, incessant sex. It seemed to him that two human beings who actually mauled each other as frequently as Chet and Fiona did would have fatal heart attacks within days of meeting. But if sex was what romance readers wanted, he felt certain he could be just as inventive as the next writer.

Second, he could see that producing something comparable to *Ivy League Lust* would be a breeze for a serious writer with his training. To begin with, there was obviously no need to labor for days, weeks, or months developing an intricate plot. It was clear that author Marcy Yum had not spent more than two minutes on hers. Chet and Fiona meet, Chet and Fiona salivate, Chet and Fiona have sex when not attending class. That was the plot in a nutshell.

Something else Grant found instructive was the writing itself. Apparently aware that her readers didn't like words containing more than two syllables, Marcy Yum loaded the book with as many monosyllabic words as she could, relying heavily on those with only four letters. From the perspective of a former English professor, *Ivy League Lust* appeared to have been written at a fifth-grade reading level for an audience that didn't care in the least about incidentals like misspellings, clumsy language, or butchered punctuation.

In a sense, this so-called novel was a comic book minus the pictures, and its sole purpose was to stimulate the sexual appetites of its readers. And there were a great many of those. *Ivy League Lust* had nearly forty thousand online reviews with an average rating of 4.7 stars.

Grant had no trouble doing the math. If he made three dollars per book and sold forty thousand copies, he would earn nearly three times what Hickston had paid him for an entire year's effort. And if he turned out three books per year, well, he would be rich in no time.

His excitement ratcheted up quickly when he stumbled across an online article indicating that only five percent of readers actually take the time to review a book. If true, that meant Marcy Yum had sold eight hundred thousand copies of *Ivy League Lust*. Assuming a profit of three dollars per book, she had earned nearly two and a half million dollars for a novel Grant knew he could replicate without breaking a sweat.

In a flash, the doorway to his future opened before him like the gates of heaven itself. Once he had banked a few million from writing pure trash, he told himself, he would exit the romance world and go back to writing the great American novel. Enough money would allow him to put the memory of his failed academic career behind him forever.

He settled onto the sumptuous upholstered recliner in Naomi's living room, opened his laptop, and created a new Word document. He gave his first romance novel the working title *Professors in Heat* and then began jotting down ideas for his two main characters.

The first protagonist was Jannah Grapple, the insatiably slutty chair of the English department at Hicksley College, who had never met someone she wasn't willing to take to bed. The second was the college's vice president for development, Albert Spool, who spent most evenings admiring himself in the bedroom mirror while attired in silk lingerie. Grant had already decided he would send autographed copies of the novel to Hannah Grackle and Arthur Sproull as soon as it was published.

With the core attributes of his key characters firmly established, he began typing the first chapter at slightly more than sixty words per minute. The story opened with late-afternoon sunlight streaming through an office window onto Professor Grapple and Buck Ruff, Hicksley's head groundskeeper, both of whom were atop her desk groping each other like frantic hyenas. A young English department lecturer, ten minutes early for his scheduled appointment with the department chairperson, opened the unlocked door, apologized for the embarrassing intrusion, and turned to leave. Grapple, however, ordered him to close the door and remain. She would be ready for him shortly.

Blessed with a sharp eye and a wicked wit, Grant described Jannah Grapple with devastating accuracy. Her shrill voice, her empty smile, and her short, thick body—*like a plump chimpanzee without all the hair*, he wrote—were rendered with remarkable clarity over the first twenty-five hundred words of *Professors in Heat*. Anyone who knew Hannah Grackle would not need to be told that she and Jannah Grapple were one and the same.

Chapter two took place in Albert Spool's home, where night had fallen and all the shades had been drawn tight. An X-rated movie, one he had watched more than a dozen times, filled the screen of his seventy-five-inch Samsung TV while he practiced putting on the living room carpet. He wore a sheer hot-pink teddy trimmed with black lace, pink Adidas golf shoes, and pink glitter lipstick. His bald head was covered by a curly pink wig that flowed over his shoulders and, at least in his mind, made him look like Lady Godiva, his favorite historical figure.

Spool rushed to the front door when the bell rang and put his eye to the peephole. He smiled and opened the door for his latest lover, who wore an expensive brown-and-white husky dog fursuit. The husky pawed lewdly at Spool before trotting to the living room, bounding onto the couch, and waiting on all fours for the fun to begin.

Grant picked up his cell phone and scrolled to the photo he had taken in Arthur Sproull's office several weeks earlier and made sure he got all the details correct. Sproull stood only five-seven, an unfortunate height for someone who weighed one hundred and ninety pounds, and gave the impression of having been built upside down because of his narrow shoulders and wide hips. Pale and jowly, he had tiny pig's eyes and overly full lips that gave him the appearance of a giant grouper preparing to swallow a hook.

The chapter ended with Spool and the husky chasing each other around the house in varying stages of undress while the grunts and moans from the TV fueled their animal appetites.

Grant checked the word count and grinned. Two chapters, nearly five thousand words. A roaring success. At that pace he could finish a first draft in twenty days or less. He went to the kitchen, grabbed a bottle of Sam Adams Summer Ale from the fridge, and toasted the day's work.

He might not be writing the great American novel, he mused, but he was well on his way to ringing the cash register big time.

22.

Les Bois wasn't just the best restaurant in Highland Falls. It was by the far the most expensive, with prices rivaling those of the finest Manhattan eateries. But tonight money was no object, thanks to Naomi's generous gift certificate.

They shared a table for two by a long window that offered a stunning view of the Hudson River, where several sailboats belonging to the West Point sailing team slowly worked their way toward the marina in the late-day light. The military academy was less than a half mile north of the restaurant.

A tiny flame flickered in a crystal candle holder at the center of the white linen tablecloth as Grant and Naomi toasted each other with glasses of Domaine Laroche Chablis and listened to the waiter describe the evening's specials. After a few moments of patient deliberation, Miranda chose the duck à l'orange and Grant opted for the filet mignon au poivre.

"So tell me about today's writing," Miranda said when they were alone again. "Did it go well?"

"Nearly five thousand words," he announced proudly, "which is a lot more than I had anticipated. With my short stories, I was lucky to get five or six hundred a day."

"Why do you suppose that is?"

"I spent most of my time thinking about character development in the short stories, but the novel is basically all about action."

His explanation struck her as rather odd. A romance novel, it seemed to her, ought to focus primarily on what happens inside the main characters' heads. Any action in the novel would therefore be secondary to the thoughts and conversations that slowly guided two people to the altar. But before she could press Grant on this point, the waiter placed a dish of butter and a basket of warm bread on the table, and that put an end to the discussion.

The bread was followed by two stunning entrées and a glorious dessert sampler consisting of an apple tart, lava chocolate cake, crème brûlée, and raspberry sorbet. It was nearly nine o'clock by the time they finished the leisurely meal, and Naomi's gift certificate covered all but ten dollars of the final tab.

"Now it's back to grilled cheese sandwiches until my books begin selling," Grant laughed as they began the twelve-minute drive back to Steinville in Naomi's fancy Mercedes. "That's about the limit of my cooking skills."

"Seriously? You don't cook much?"

He shook his head. "Grilled cheese, spaghetti with Newman's Own marinara, and scrambled eggs are about it. How about you? Do you like to cook?"

"I enjoy it a lot. Usually nothing complicated, but I cook three or four times a week."

"What's your favorite meal?"

She thought for a moment. "Bouillabaisse, I guess. It takes forever, so I don't make it often. But when I do, it's always a hit."

"I've only had it once, and I loved it."

"Then I'll make it for you sometime."

Is it true, she wondered, that the way to a man's heart is through his stomach? She was skeptical but willing to test the theory.

Grant slowed the car as he approached Miranda's home.

"I've been thinking," he said, turning to her with a smile.

"What have you been thinking?" she asked enticingly. It seemed for a moment that the lovely dinner for two might have succeeded in turning his attention to romance.

"That you shouldn't have to mess with Rajah's litter box after a fancy meal like that. Why don't you just show me how to do it tomorrow?"

She fought the urge to scream. For most of her life she had battled men who believed that taking her to a movie or buying her dinner entitled them to sex on demand, but Grant seemed not to pick up on her obvious overtures. Was he gay? Celibate? Terminally clueless?

"That's very thoughtful of you," she said with great restraint, "but I'm sure it needs to be done tonight. I'll show you how, and then the job is all yours. How's that?"

"Are you sure?"

"I'm positive. Let's go."

When they reached Naomi's, they walked through the kitchen and down into the basement, where Miranda spent thirty seconds cleaning the litter box.

Grant was pleasantly surprised. "That's all there is to it?"

"Uh, huh. Not so bad, right?"

"No, not at all. Thank you. I can definitely handle this," he said, following her up the stairs.

"I'm confident you can. Now, since it's still early, how about we go into the living room and get comfortable?"

Something about the way she said *get comfortable* made it sound like an invitation to something more, but he was afraid he had misheard. The last thing he wanted to do was move too quickly with a woman he was growing quite fond of.

"Sure," he said. "That sounds nice."

Unfortunately, the idea of getting comfortable vanished when they reached the kitchen and found Rajah sitting on the granite island with a small furry object in his mouth. Miranda gasped.

"Please say that's not a mouse, Grant."

"That's not a mouse, Grant."

She elbowed him gently in the ribs. "It *is* a mouse!"

"Of course, it is. The long tail was a giveaway."

"I can't deal with mice."

"They don't bite, Miranda."

"I was bitten by a mouse when I was five."

"I stand corrected."

"Please get rid of it," she said nervously.

He turned to Rajah and in a deep voice yelled, "Drop the mouse!" Surprisingly, the cat did as he was told. Also surprisingly, the mouse stopped playing dead, leapt off the island, and scurried under the Viking refrigerator with Rajah in hot pursuit.

Miranda slowly retreated to the far corner of the kitchen while Grant began searching feverishly through cabinet drawers.

"What are you looking for?" she asked in an uncharacteristically high-pitched voice.

"A flashlight."

"Why?"

"I want to see if there's a hole in the wall behind the refrigerator."

"Why?"

"Because if there's a hole, maybe the mouse is already gone."

"Oh."

He found the flashlight hanging on a hook in the pantry, flicked it on, and flopped on the floor next to Rajah, who was growling and pawing wildly under the refrigerator. The mouse was all the way back, almost to the wall, calmly nibbling on what appeared to be a scrap of dried bread. It blinked when the beam of light hit it, then turned its back to the intruder.

"It's there," Grant reported.

"So how do we get rid of it?"

"First you need to get the cat out of here. Then I'll decide what to do with the mouse."

Rajah wasn't happy about leaving the kitchen, but he offered only modest resistance when Miranda picked him up and carried him to the master bedroom. She closed the door behind them and locked it. Grant, meanwhile, returned to the kitchen cabinets in search of a container suitable for imprisoning a house mouse. On the shelf of an upper cabinet he found a plastic bowl with a snap-on lid, thereby solving the easy part of his problem. The hard part would be getting the mouse to enter the container and remain there while the lid was secured.

Grant's first strategy was to place a spoonful of leftover quiche in the container, set it near the base of the refrigerator, and stand back. When that failed, he scooped some peanut butter in the container and tried again with the same result.

Forty minutes later, his frustration growing, he took a more forceful direct approach. He reached under the refrigerator with a wooden yard stick and swung it back and forth until the mouse decided to leave its cozy hiding place. The mouse ran past Grant, through the kitchen, and into the foyer, where it squeezed under the door of the coat closet, trapping itself. It nevertheless took Grant another twenty minutes to back the mouse into a corner and place the plastic container over it upside down.

"I got it!" he yelled to Miranda.

When Miranda opened the bedroom door, Rajah raced out, found Grant in the foyer, and pounced on the overturned container, releasing the mouse. A few seconds later, the mouse was safely under the Viking refrigerator once again.

The next time Grant caught the mouse—which happened to be at 11:50 p.m.—he waited until he had taken it outside and released it in the backyard before telling Miranda the coast was clear.

"You're sure it's gone?" she asked after joining him in the kitchen.

Rajah was plainly wondering the same thing. He looked under the refrigerator, sniffed his way through the coat closet, and prowled from one end of the house to the other, unwilling to give up the hunt.

"It's gone, Miranda. I took it out back and let it go."

She looked warily toward the back door. "But what if it gets back inside?"

"Then Rajah's in charge. He was doing fine until we got involved." He glanced at his watch. "I should probably take you home."

"I'm beat," she admitted, "and you probably are too."

The drive to Miranda's home took all of two minutes. Before getting out of the car, she leaned over and gave him a quick kiss on the cheek.

"Thank you for dinner and for hunting down the mouse," she said. "Despite the attack, I had a good time.."

He grinned. "So did I. I guess I'll see you when you get back from your conference?"

"That's a promise."

After waiting until she had gone into the house and locked the door, he drove back to Naomi's. It was a few minutes after midnight when he walked into the kitchen and discovered Rajah on the kitchen island looking pleased with himself. A wriggling mouse hung from his mouth.

"Good boy," Grant said before turning the light off and going to bed.

23.

Grant fell into a comfortable and productive routine while Miranda was attending her three-day conference at Harvard. He woke each morning at 6:30 sharp when Rajah jumped onto the bed and purred like a motorcycle until being fed. After that, he hit Naomi's well-equipped home fitness center for twenty minutes on the weight machine and treadmill, then showered and ate a light breakfast of spoon-size shredded wheat with two-percent milk. Finally, he spent forty-five minutes watering, misting, feeding, and deadheading all the plants listed on Naomi's rigorous schedule before sitting down with his laptop.

He began writing no later than 9:00 a.m. and worked straight through until noon, when he took a short lunch before writing again until 4:30 or 5:00. To his astonishment, he was able to average more than eight thousand words per day despite the challenges of caring for Rajah and Naomi's indoor-outdoor plant farm. In fact, he discovered that time spent with the cat, plants, flowers, and shrubs was unexpectedly relaxing. Caring for something other than his own needs turned out to be a satisfying way to start the day, and he believed it helped explain his exceptional productivity.

Whatever the reason, *Professors in Heat* was practically writing itself. Grant could see and feel his fingers gliding across the keyboard, but the words seemed to appear magically on the screen without his conscious involvement. Freed of the technical concerns that serious authors spend lifetimes fretting over—plotting, character development, word choice, and a host of similar impediments—he simply allowed the story to leap from one sexploit to the next. *Professors in Heat* was all about action, and the action was nonstop.

Professor Jannah Grapple wasted as little time as possible on academic matters so that she could indulge her prodigious sexual appetites page after page, chapter after chapter. Professors, deans, coaches, students, groundskeepers, deliverymen, and even members of Hickston's board of trustees succumbed to her overtures, often in the oddest places. Although she was partial to upscale hotels, she was willing and able to perform capably in offices, elevators, locker rooms, delivery trucks, tents, and, naturally, the back seats of cars. Beach dunes, shady woods, and swimming pools also made her list of favorite places as long as the weather was reasonably accommodating.

Albert Spool, meanwhile, considered himself an enlightened pansexual who ignored all accepted norms when choosing his partners, most of them with two legs rather than four. Nevertheless, he was far more skilled than Jannah Grapple when it came to keeping his prurient interests under wraps, and he never experimented on campus or with anyone even remotely affiliated with the college. He reserved his licentious behavior for his own home and for a handful of discreet clubs that catered to patrons whose sexual preferences were well outside the bounds of what most humans considered normal.

By the time *Professors in Heat* reached thirty thousand words, Grant had reimagined Hannah Grackle and Arthur Sproull in ruthless detail, flawlessly blending their fictional behavior with masterful recreations of their looks, speech, and mannerisms. He even captured the odd quirks that people who knew them would recognize instantly. For Grackle it was the way her left eye twitched whenever she was mad. For Sproull it was the way he drummed his fingers on his desk when agitated.

Grant briefly worried that his descriptions of Grapple and Spool might be so accurate as to allow Grackle and Sproull to sue him over the caricatures. But the moment passed. Like all novels, *Professors in Heat* would clearly state up front that all the characters were figments of the author's imagination and that any resemblance to real persons was inadvertent. If that was good enough for every other writer in America, it was surely good enough for him. Besides, Grackle and Sproull had earned his enmity and richly deserved the savage double-barreled treatment.

Miranda phoned him at 7:30 the night before she was to leave Massachusetts, and they had a brief but pleasant conversation. Yes, he told her, everything was fine at Naomi's. He hadn't killed the plants yet, and the cat was being properly brushed and fed.

"How about the mouse?" she asked.

"The mouse is gone," he assured her. He didn't mention the tail that Rajah had left behind on the kitchen island following his late-night snack. The garbage disposal had eliminated that unpleasant scrap of evidence. "How's your conference?"

"Fairly depressing, unfortunately. Unless you teach Spanish or Chinese, you're headed for extinction. If I were looking for a new job teaching French right now, I'd be out of luck."

"You should be a college president anyway. But we've already had that conversation, haven't we?"

"Yes, we have. So how's the writing?"

She was jolted by the news that Grant had already written more than thirty thousand words over seventeen chapters. Even the most prolific of novelists would have been hard pressed to match that output, and she couldn't shake the feeling that he must be taking shortcuts with the process. She was annoyed with herself for not having pursued the topic when they dined at Les Bois together, so she was pleased with what he said next.

"Maybe you can read it when you get home and see what you think. I did some market research, as you suggested, but this romance stuff is new to me, and I want to make sure I'm on the right track."

"I'm sure you are," she said doubtfully, not wishing to dent his enthusiasm, "but I'd be happy to look it over tomorrow."

Miranda said she would leave Harvard after listening to the final luncheon address, and the drive home would take no more than four hours. They agreed they would probably go out for dinner when she arrived.

Grant was surprised when his cell phone rang again a half hour later because he rarely got calls, but he broke out in a wide grin when he checked the caller ID and saw who was calling.

It had been far too long since he had spoken with Lisa.

24.

The next day Grant deviated from his strict writing routine. Instead of creating new material for *Professors in Heat*, he spent the entire morning polishing the first thirty thousand words so that Miranda wouldn't have to struggle with the endless typos. Assuming she liked what she saw, he would bang out another forty thousand words, do some revising, and self-publish the book on Amazon. After that, all he had to do was invest in a little post-publication advertising and wait for the royalties to pour in.

He broke for lunch and made himself a tuna salad sandwich, part of which he fed in sizable chunks to Rajah, who had gotten into the habit of sitting on the kitchen floor and begging whenever Grant ate. Since Naomi's detailed instructions had not touched on the issue of feeding the cat table scraps, Grant assumed doing so was acceptable. Besides, it was the only way to keep Rajah from growling at him throughout the entire meal.

After lunch he spent two hours searching through stock photography websites to find an image that might be suitable for his novel's cover. After viewing hundreds of photos, he found two that had enormous potential. The first showed a well-endowed pole dancer partially covered by a stripper's minimalist version of an academic gown. She leered at the audience while men waved five-dollar bills at her. Although Jannah Grapple had not yet done any pole dancing in the novel, Grant could easily take care of that detail with a few short paragraphs. Jannah was, after all, a woman of limitless talents.

The second photo showed a man and a woman, presumably Jannah Grapple and Albert Spool, groping each other while wearing animal costumes. The woman was dressed as a pink fox, the man as a panda. What they intended to do was clear. How they intended to do it while outfitted in their furry finery remained a question.

His thoughts were interrupted by the sound of a car pulling into the driveway, and he rushed outside to greet Lisa, who was stepping from the driver's seat of a classic metallic-red Maserati GranTurismo convertible. She had golden hair that cascaded over her shoulders, a smile bright enough to rival the sun, and a body that several years earlier had graced the cover of *Sports Illustrated* clad only in a string bikini. Today she wore a white nine-hundred-dollar T-shirt and a twelve-hundred-dollar floral miniskirt, both by Dolce & Gabbana, and delicate Gucci sandals that had cost another six hundred dollars.

Because she was quite a bit shorter than Grant, she stood on her tiptoes as they held each other tight. Several months had passed since their last embrace at a resort in Bermuda, and the hug felt remarkably like home. They spoke the same words at the same moment: "I missed you."

The last thing Miranda had expected to see when she turned into Naomi's driveway was Grant with his arms wrapped around a long-haired blonde whose perfect butt was not quite fully covered by her microscopic miniskirt. Miranda's hands tightened around the steering wheel as she decided whether to back out and leave gracefully or to hit the gas and run Grant and his lover down where they stood.

Then she allowed reason to set in. She forced herself to admit that whatever so-called relationship she and Grant shared was in her head, not his. It was now obvious that he had kept her at arm's length because he was involved with someone else. Someone who dressed like a starlet and drove a car that had probably cost more than the average American home.

She had just put the BMW in reverse when Grant looked up, smiled, and waved to her. Then the blonde did the same. The two of them brazenly stood there side by side, apparently waiting for her to join them. Fine, she thought. I'll say hello, leave, and never think about Grant Hunter again.

As Miranda was pulling up the long driveway, Lisa popped the Maserati's trunk and lifted out an elegant Michael Kors overnight bag and set it on the ground, a signal that she was moving in. *Dear Naomi. Grant has a high-priced whore living with him in your house. I'm sure they'll enjoy the vibrating bed.*

When Miranda stopped the car, Grant opened the door for her and casually said, "I have a big surprise for you."

"Oh, how I love surprises," she muttered between clenched teeth.

Miranda's jaw nearly hit the ground when the blonde walked over, extended her beautiful hand, and said, "Hi, I'm Lisa Hunter."

Recognition flashed in Miranda's eyes. "I've seen you on a magazine cover, haven't I?"

"She's on lots of magazine covers," Grant chimed in. "My big sister is one of the world's top models. And she's here for one night before jetting off for the luxurious French Riviera."

"He makes it sound like a vacation," Lisa said offhandedly, "but it's not. I'll probably work ten hours a day while I'm in France. Then I go right on to London for more of the same."

"You should take things a little easier," Grant said sternly, grabbing the overnight bag, "now that money is no longer an issue."

"More money is better than less money," Lisa countered, "especially since my days of earning top dollar as a model are almost over. I'm already thinking about what comes next."

"Any idea yet what that might be?" Miranda asked as they walked toward the front door.

Lisa thought for a moment. "I have ideas for my own clothing line, but at this point I'm still keeping my options wide open."

They entered the house and were passing through the foyer jungle when Rajah sprang from behind an immense elephant ear plant and raced toward the kitchen.

"Oh, my God, what a beautiful cat!" Lisa exclaimed. "Is he yours, Grant?"

"No, actually this is his house, and I'm nothing more than the resident feeder. As you can tell, he knows it's time for dinner."

"Speaking of dinner," Miranda said, "I stopped at a fish market in Boston on the way home and packed a cooler bag with everything I need to make bouillabaisse in case anyone's interested."

She was puzzled when Grant and Lisa looked at each other and laughed.

"The last time Grant and I saw each other," Lisa explained, "was at the Cafe Lido in Bermuda, and we both ordered the bouillabaisse."

"And we both said we could probably eat it every day for the rest of our lives. Well, in my case, until the money ran out."

"Perfect," Miranda said. "I'll get the fish while you guys take care of Rajah."

"No, I'll come with you," Lisa protested. "I'm the world's worst cook, so at least let me carry the food in before I eat it."

Miranda smiled. "Deal."

As they walked to the car, Lisa turned to Miranda and said, "Grant told me you were in Cambridge for a few days. That may be my favorite city on the planet."

The comment took Miranda totally by surprise. For a supermodel who had spent her life in some of the world's most exotic places to pronounce Cambridge her favorite city was wholly unexpected.

"We're talking about Cambridge, Massachusetts, right? Not Cambridge, England."

Lisa nodded. "I got my undergraduate degree from MIT in history, and I loved living in Cambridge. At one point I thought I'd stay there and become a college professor." She hoisted the cooler bag from the trunk. "Then my part-time modeling work sort of took off, and here I am, ready to learn how to make bouillabaisse."

Miranda shook her head in amazement. "A supermodel with an MIT degree and a brother who never told me anything about her."

"He would have gotten around to it eventually. In case you haven't noticed, he tends to be rather shy."

"I *have* noticed. I thought maybe, well, I'm not really sure exactly what I thought."

"You thought maybe he didn't like you. But he does. Quite a lot, actually."

Dear Naomi. Please delete the message about the high-priced whore.

25.

Miranda had spent a small fortune on lobster, haddock, shrimp, clams, mussels, and scallops, all of which had been caught that same day in the Atlantic off the coast of Massachusetts. The cooler bag also contained a variety of other necessary ingredients, everything from onions to saffron, that would help produce one of the world's most beloved seafood dishes if properly orchestrated.

While she and Lisa laid the food out on the kitchen counter, Grant explored the pantry to see whether Naomi had left a bottle of wine behind. She had. He walked over to the women with a bottle of merlot in his hand.

Miranda and Lisa looked at each other, smiled, and shook their heads in unison.

"We're going to need something white," Miranda declared, leaving no room for doubt.

"And it must be French," Lisa insisted, "if we're going to have an authentic French meal."

"How many bottles?" Grant asked.

"Two should be fine," Miranda said. "We want to save some room for the bouillabaisse, right?"

"Definitely," said Lisa. "Plus, I'd prefer not to be hung over when I fly to France tomorrow."

"Okay, two bottles of French white coming up. Just make sure you don't talk about me behind my back," Grant joked as he left the kitchen.

"We wouldn't think of it, baby brother," Lisa snickered.

The talking began as soon as he closed the door on his way out.

Lisa told Miranda that her father, now sixty-seven and retired, had taught his son and daughter to support each other unconditionally, and they had always done so. Their mother, also retired, had spent her life as an outspoken supporter of women's rights and now served as a member of a local women's business council. Given this sort of upbringing, Lisa said, it was only natural for Grant to be excessively protective of his older but smaller sister. From elementary school right on through high school, if anyone messed with Lisa or her friends, Grant was prepared to bloody someone's nose and risk having his own nose bloodied in return.

"But his protectiveness had a downside," Lisa noted. "Because he understood that girls were often mistreated, he was determined never to be part of the problem. So when he was in high school, just asking someone for a date made him feel he might be overstepping his bounds. As far as I know, the only time he dated was if a girl asked him."

The pieces of the puzzle finally snapped into place for Miranda.

"That's what you meant earlier when you said he's shy."

"*Shy* is hardly the word for it. But, yes, that's what I meant. He thinks you're special, Miranda, and it's easy to see why. But if you're waiting for him to take the initiative, you have a long wait ahead of you."

"Message received."

"Good. Then how about that bouillabaisse lesson?"

"Absolutely."

By the time Grant returned home, the kitchen smelled like a fine French restaurant, and Rajah was impatiently pacing the floor waiting for a piece of fish to jump into his mouth.

"I guess cats like bouillabaisse," he said, placing two bottles of wine on the counter. "If he behaves during dinner, maybe he'll get some fish."

"And if you give the chefs some wine," Lisa added, "maybe you'll get to taste some bouillabaisse."

Grant uncorked the first bottle of Chateau Coucheroy sauvignon blanc and poured three glasses. Miranda raised hers and said, "*Bon voyage, Lisa.*"

"*À toi et Grant,*" Lisa replied. To you and Grant.

"I understood *bon voyage,*" Grant said, "but I didn't catch the second toast."

"Your French has always been terrible, baby brother. I'm not sure you're qualified to eat bouillabaisse."

"No bouillabaisse for me, no more wine for you," he fired back.

"*Touché.*"

"*Sommes-nous prêts à manger?*" Miranda asked.

"I understood *manger,*" Grant replied, "and that's all I care about."

"I asked whether we're all ready to eat."

"*Oui.* I'll set the table."

While Miranda was giving the bouillabaisse one final stir, she watched Grant put out three large bowls and then neatly place the silverware alongside them. Forks to the left on top of napkins, knives and soup spoons to the right. She was impressed. Her ex-husband had known that the silverware was kept in a drawer somewhere in the kitchen, but that had been the limit of his interest. Actually setting a table was something he had never tried.

The bouillabaisse was fabulous, and the reason for that soon became clear. Miranda had spent a year in France as an undergraduate and had vacationed there no fewer than a dozen times since then. Each of those later trips, several of them as much as a month long, had been devoted to studying the language, culture, and, of course, the food of a different region. At one point she had thought about opening a French restaurant but finally decided she would not be happy doing the same thing every day of her life. Teaching allowed her to read, learn, and explore the world in ways that would never have been possible if she had been tied down by a restaurant.

"It also seemed to me that being a professor would provide greater job security," she observed a bit sadly, "but that has turned out not to be the case. Hickston College has real financial problems, and if things get bad enough, even tenured faculty positions will be at risk."

"Self-employment has its downside," Lisa said, "but I wouldn't trade it for anything. I get to decide what jobs I'll take or decline, and I set the rules on what kind of work I'm willing to do." She turned to Grant. "I know that not getting tenure was a disappointment, but I think you'll be better off devoting yourself fully to writing. You'll be terrific."

"I hope you're right. I'm having fun so far," he said, "but that's partly because I have someone else's roof over my head."

"Work hard and be honest," Lisa said. "Sound familiar?"

"That's Dad's mantra. If you work hard and stay honest, everything will work out."

"Makes sense to me," Miranda said. "It's nice to have a little good luck thrown in now and then, but I believe hard work and honesty should be enough."

Grant hoped she was right. Hard work and honesty hadn't brought him success as an academic, but perhaps they would prove more effective in his budding career as a romance author.

They spent the remainder of the evening on the screened porch finishing the wine and, perhaps inspired by the bouillabaisse, talking mostly about France. It turned out that Lisa had visited France even more frequently than Miranda though never for more than a few days at a time. Grant had spent only two days in Paris while on his way back to the U.S. from England, and what he remembered most vividly was mistakenly ordering calf sweetbreads for dinner at a popular cafe.

"I saw *ris de veau* on the menu," he said, "and knew that *veau* meant veal. So I thought I was ordering veal scallopini or something. Turns out . . ."

"That *ris de veau* is actually veal pancreas," Lisa laughed. "My poor baby brother. Next time you go to France, take Miranda and let her order." She glanced at her watch and saw that it was nearly 10:00. "I have a long day ahead of me tomorrow, so I'm going to turn in early. It was lovely meeting you," she said to Miranda. "I hope we'll see each other again soon."

"I'm looking forward to it," Miranda replied. "Travel safely."

After Lisa had gone to bed, Grant said, "I had a great time tonight, and the meal was amazing."

"Thanks. This was a lot of fun. You have a wonderful sister, and I can't believe how down-to-earth she is. It's certainly not what I expected."

"Modesty and honesty go hand in hand."

"Another one of your father's mantras?"

He smiled. "My mother's, actually."

"Well, she's right." Miranda hesitated for a moment, then asked a question that had been on her mind for the past several days. "Day after tomorrow Farnsworth is having a reception at his house for senior faculty members, and I was wondering if you would go with me."

His pained expression left little doubt about what he was thinking.

"That could be uncomfortable in light of what happened with my accidental tenure announcement."

"More uncomfortable for Farnsworth than for you, I would think, but if you don't want to go, I'll just cancel. I don't want to go alone." She could tell he was wavering. "The weather will be great, and we'll have a good time. If you absolutely hate it, we can escape early."

"You're sure?"

"Absolutely. I promise."

"Okay, I'll go."

"Thanks, Grant. And now it's time for me to go home. I'm beat."

As they walked to her car, Grant asked whether he could email her a Word file containing the first thirty thousand words of his romance novel. He felt he was on the right track but would really appreciate her opinion.

"Send it before you go to bed," she said, "and I'll read it first thing in the morning. I can't wait."

Her enthusiasm made him feel even more confident about what he had written so far, and he looked forward to her critique.

Why, he wondered, had he wasted so much time working for a living when he could have been writing romances?

26.

Lisa left for Manhattan right after breakfast to spend time with her agent and then have lunch with two friends before departing for Paris. Grant waved to her from the driveway as she drove off with the Maserati's top down, and he puzzled over the last words she had spoken: "Miranda's the one, little brother. Don't blow it."

Both statements were baffling. How could his sister think Miranda was *the one* after spending only a few hours with her? And what exactly did she mean by *don't blow it?* After all these years surely Lisa knew he would never behave badly with any woman. So what was she afraid he might do to damage his friendship with Miranda? Nearly an hour later, after misting and watering Naomi's indoor jungle, he was still wondering.

At 10:00 a.m. he drove into Steinville to pick up some groceries, mostly bachelor-style items that could be prepared quickly and with minimal fuss. Tuna fish, canned chili, and sliced American cheese accounted for most of the short shopping list. On a whim he also bought ground beef and a package of hamburger buns, thinking he would invite Miranda over for lunch after she finished reviewing his manuscript.

He was heading toward the checkout counter when he spotted Juliet Swanson walking down the aisle toward him. Next to her was the Hickston football team's star linebacker, Neander Slunk, a gifted athlete with the IQ of a lima bean. The sneer on Juliet's face indicated she was still angry over not getting the A she hadn't deserved.

Grant nodded and attempted to walk by, but Juliet blocked his path while Neander glared at him like a Rottweiler whose bone had been stolen.

"I'd like to sign up for one of your classes next semester," Juliet said sarcastically. "Oh, wait, you got fired, didn't you?" Then she and Neander laughed as they continued on their way. Neander made a point of slamming his rock-hard shoulder into Grant when they passed each other.

The unpleasant supermarket encounter was still uppermost in Grant's mind when he returned to Naomi's house and walked into a kitchen that resembled a war zone. Rajah had clawed his way into the cabinet beneath the sink and pulled out the black trash bag containing the remains of the previous night's meal. Lobster shells, shrimp tails, and smelly plastic bags from the Boston seafood market had been tossed indiscriminately with scraps of onion, garlic, and tomato across the entire floor. When the cat caught the murderous look in Grant's eyes, he grabbed a reeking lobster shell with his teeth and ran toward the living room.

After spending thirty minutes clearing the debris and mopping the floor with Lysol, Grant began searching for the cat and the missing lobster shell. Finding Rajah was easy. He was lying in a sunbeam alongside a potted fern, licking his paws and ignoring the human interloper. Locating the lobster shell proved impossible, however, despite a long and increasingly frantic search. In the end, Grant assumed Rajah had eaten the shell and would soon die. That's the kind of day it had been.

The bad day got even worse when he took Miranda's call shortly before noon. She seemed agitated and said they needed to talk about the manuscript. Sooner rather than later, she emphasized. He asked where she wanted to meet, and after a long pause she said she would come over to Naomi's. He was waiting outside for her when she showed up ten minutes later, laptop in hand and a scowl on her face.

"Is everything okay?" he asked as she marched past him toward the front door.

"No, Grant, everything's not okay," she said over her shoulder.

He followed her to the living room and waited for her to sit on the couch. When he tried to sit alongside her, she pointed to an armchair on the opposite side of the coffee table. He went there and sat without saying a word.

"I'm not going to ask what you were thinking about while you were writing," she began, "because that much is obvious. What I'm wondering is why you thought any civilized human being would want to read something like this."

"A romance?"

"You call this a romance? This is a sex-education manual for apes. I quit reading after ten pages of throbbing, panting, groping, moaning, thrusting, pawing, and salivating. I thought you did some research."

"I did," he said defensively. "I read a top-selling romance and wrote something in the same style."

"What did you read, Grant?"

"*Ivy League Lust* by Marcy Yum."

"Marcy Yum? Seriously?"

"Uh, huh. I can show it to you."

Miranda put her hands up defensively. "No, I don't need to read anything by someone who calls herself Marcy Yum. If you were going to do market research, why didn't you read something by Nora Roberts, who probably sells more romance novels than anyone else on earth?"

"Because her books were a lot more expensive, and I figured a romance is a romance."

"What you've written isn't a romance, Grant. It's called pornography, and I wouldn't want to live on the planet you've described. There's no human connection whatsoever. Body parts touch and touch and touch. That's it." She paused to regain her composure. "In my opinion, the people who are most likely to read this sort of thing are in prison cells."

"I thought I was following your advice," he said softly, a wounded half-smile on his lips. "I apologize if I've offended you."

That he was completely crushed was obvious to Miranda. Also obvious was that she had failed to give sufficient guidance to someone who apparently knew almost nothing about romance, either in a book or in real life. She had told him to follow the style of what was already selling well in the marketplace, and that's precisely what he had done. Now she blamed herself for not having told him specifically what to read. Left to his own devices, he had stumbled upon the darkest corner of the erotic romance genre and wasted thirty thousand words on his own version.

"You haven't offended me, Grant. You simply went off in the wrong direction, and I take responsibility for that. I should have spent more time talking with you about the romance genre and helping you find the right niche. The good news," she said brightly, "is that you're an excellent writer, so all we have to do is set you on the right path."

"You think the writing is okay?"

"No, I think your writing is excellent. It's the subject matter that's terribly wrong. We can fix this."

They continued the discussion on the back patio while Grant fired up the Weber grill. Miranda explained that the romance genre actually consists of several major subgenres—contemporary, historical, religious, suspense, paranormal, young adult, and, of course, erotic—each of which can be broken down even further to reach a highly specific audience.

"For example, someone who loves Victorian romances," she said, "might not like medieval romances, even though they're both in the historical genre. So if you're going to write romances, you need to consider the size of the audience as well as what sort of love story interests you most."

"The only love stories I'm familiar with are either from Arthurian legend—Lancelot and Guinevere, for instance—or Shakespeare's plays, which in all honesty I never cared for."

"An English professor who never cared for Shakespeare. Now that's a first," she said, following him into the kitchen to help form the hamburgers.

"An *ex* English professor who thinks Shakespeare's plays are deathly boring."

"Yet still extremely popular."

"Only because students are forced to read them."

"Okay, back to love stories. Did you not read *Jane Eyre?*"

He walked outside and tossed four burgers on the grill. "I've never even thought about reading *Jane Eyre.*"

"*Wuthering Heights?*"

He shook his head.

"*Gone With the Wind?*"

"Saw half the movie and hated it."

"*The Great Gatsby?*"

"I can't stand Fitzgerald."

"*Anna Karenina?*"

"I don't read Russian authors."

"How about movies?" she finally asked. "Surely you've seen love movies."

"I like action and adventure. Sci-fi now and then, but mostly action and adventure. I actually haven't seen many movies because I prefer to watch sports on TV."

Miranda tabled the discussion while they ate all four burgers—three for him, one for her—but she took an entirely different approach as soon as they were finished with lunch.

"Tell me a little about your personal experience with love."

He stared off in space, pondering what Miranda had assumed was a simple question. After great deliberation he said, "I dated a girl for about a month during my junior year of college, but she was a little too serious. Actually, she was way too serious."

"Meaning what?"

"Meaning she was thinking about getting married, and I was thinking about graduating and then going on for a master's degree. Having a wife and kids wasn't on my mind."

"Okay, who else?"

He shook his head. "No one else. I had dates now and then, but I certainly wasn't in love with anyone."

Miranda's smile masked a growing sense of panic. At her urging, a man who had never been in love had decided to become a romance writer, and she had offered to help.

It was now fairly obvious there was no way this could end well.

27.

The annual year-end reception for senior faculty members was always the highlight of President Farnsworth's social calendar. It gave him an opportunity to take full credit for all achievements and to blame any shortcomings on staff members since they were not invited to the event. When the weather cooperated, the event was held outdoors, and on this particular day the weather was behaving kindly. The temperature was eighty-two at noon when the reception began, the coolers were overflowing with bottles of beer and wine, and the steaks were already hitting the five grills that had been placed strategically around the president's house.

The mansion was surrounded by mature shrubs of every description and flower beds thick with petunias, zinnias, hydrangeas, asters, and dahlias. Tall maples and oaks provided cooling shade from which to view the Hudson River that gleamed far below in the afternoon sunlight. There were cushioned chairs and tables draped with linen tablecloths to accommodate Farnsworth's fortunate guests, and the school's award-winning string quartet entertained everyone with music by the likes of Beethoven, Mozart, Borodin, and Haydn.

Two dozen couples were already strolling the grounds, drinks in hand, when Grant and Miranda arrived and attempted to slip into the crowd unnoticed. But Farnsworth's live-in lover, Alicia Fillip, spotted them immediately and walked over.

"It's so lovely to see you, Miranda," she said, slurring her words slightly after three glasses of excellent chardonnay, "but I don't believe I've had the pleasure of meeting your husband."

"I got divorced months ago," Miranda said casually. "This is my date, Grant Hunter."

Alicia extended her hand and smiled. "What do you do, Grant?" she asked.

"I write pornographic novels," he said with a pleasant smile just as the president joined them. Alicia looked distressed.

"I'm surprised to see you here, Grant," Farnsworth said, a long frown on his face. "To what do we owe the pleasure?"

"He's my escort," Miranda answered without hesitation.

"I see."

"Grant writes pornography, Porter," Alicia announced a bit too loudly. She took a fourth glass of chardonnay from the waiter who was passing through the crowd. After a quick gulp, she mumbled, "I've never met a pornographer before."

"Nor have I," Farnsworth said abruptly. He told Miranda to enjoy herself and led Alicia away by her elbow.

"What a bad boy you can be," Miranda whispered to Grant. Her wicked smile let him know she thought he had performed admirably.

"My parents always taught me to be honest, Miranda. She asked what I do, and I told her."

"Yes, I heard. But your pornography days are over, aren't they?"

He crossed his heart. "I promise."

After equipping themselves with drinks—chardonnay for her, Sam Adams Summer Ale for him—they began making the rounds, chatting briefly with a series of faculty acquaintances until they came across Jim McArdle and his wife Dana, an advertising executive.

"Well, if it isn't the scandalous Grant Hunter, pornographer extraordinaire," Jim chuckled.

Grant and Jim shook hands while Miranda and Dana, longtime friends, shared a hug.

"I take it you've already spoken with the president's housemate," Grant said.

"I have indeed. Farnsworth is trying to get her to keep quiet, but alcohol has loosened her tongue. Why did you tell her you're a pornographer?"

"She asked me what I do, so I had to think of something."

"It was a stroke of genius. I believe you've succeeded in ruining Porter's day."

"May it be so."

The four of them were eagerly talking about anything but Hickston College when Grackle came up the long front walk in the company of a man they had never seen before. Jim caught the grin on Grant's face.

"Don't say it," Jim warned.

"What, that they're both so ugly they belong in cages? Can you imagine what their offspring would look like?"

"God help our species."

"He looks like a troll from a bad fairy tale."

Jim studied the newcomer. "He sort of does, doesn't he?"

The man in question was short, profoundly overweight, and winded from having climbed the brick steps in front of the president's house. His ears were too small for his head and his eyes too large, giving him the appearance of an oversized lemur. He rocked from side to side as he walked, chimpanzee-style.

"There's someone for everyone," Dana said charitably, trying hard not to laugh.

"Even mutants like Grackle," Grant agreed.

When Grackle noticed Grant staring at her, she took her date by the arm and pulled him toward the opposite side of the house.

"She looks as though she smells something bad," Jim cracked.

"She's downwind of her mate."

"That would do it."

Grant was telling Jim and Dana about his new career as a romance novelist when the head caterer began walking through the crowd asking people to take their seats. Jim commandeered a shady table for four, and they spent the next hour dining on steak, baked potatoes, and grilled vegetables. The main course was followed by slabs of chocolate layer cake and platters of freshly baked cookies.

"That was distinctly better than the food at Vulture Commons," Grant observed when the meal ended.

"That's because Farnsworth hired an outside service," Jim said.

"But I did miss the brush bristles."

During a lull in the conversation, Miranda nudged Grant and called his attention to Tex and Sherry Brawner, who were standing by Farnsworth's table showing off six-month-old Brad.

"Now *that*," she said, "is the kind of story romance readers can get into."

"Tex and Sherry?"

"Yes. A young coach takes over a failing basketball program, leads the team to the national championship, and falls in love with the college's alumni director along the way."

He rolled his eyes. "And then they and their beautiful children live happily ever after. Pretty sappy stuff."

"Sappy sells better than piggish," Miranda said. "In a world filled with so many bad endings, romance readers are quite content to escape reality in love stories that end well."

"Have you ever watched the Hallmark Channel?" Dana asked Grant.

"Not that I can recall."

"Then you need to start, and I mean *tonight*. Their ad revenue is off the chart because Hallmark is *the* place to reach women on television. Watch a few Hallmark movies, and you'll know what to write."

"Okay, thanks," Grant said halfheartedly. "I'll give it a try."

Jim's unhelpful contribution to the exchange was, "There's a good Yankees game on TV tonight. They play Boston."

Dana looked at Miranda and slowly shook her head. The unspoken message was clear: men are beyond hope.

When the party ended and Grant was driving away from the campus, Miranda said, "Thanks for going with me today. I hope you didn't feel too uncomfortable."

"I felt great, actually. I think being there as a guest rather than a faculty member helped me move on. I've put Hickston behind me."

"And now you're a successful pornographer," she laughed. "I still can't believe you said that to Alicia."

"I hope I didn't make things difficult for you and Farnsworth."

"Farnsworth is a windbag who has no control over me whatsoever. Unless I murder someone, he couldn't get rid of me if he wanted to."

"And you're not going to murder anyone, are you?"

She looked at him and grinned. "I suppose that depends on what you write next."

He wasn't entirely sure she was joking.

28.

Grant spent the next two days first developing the plot for a new novel and then banging out five thousand words. The storyline was hardly unique: two men were vying for the attention of a beautiful woman, and the woman was unable to decide which of them was Mr. Right. But there were no sex scenes within the first four chapters, and that alone, Grant thought, would be enough to win Miranda's praise. He emailed her a copy of the work in progress, and she promised to stop by that afternoon to give him her thoughts.

He was nearly finished mowing the lawn when she arrived, and he was enormously proud of himself for not having accidentally eliminated Naomi's flower beds in the process. Riding around on the huge John Deere tractor was rather relaxing, he thought, and hardly constituted actual work. He was free to let his mind wander while the machine neatly cut the grass, chopped the clippings into fine bits, and mulched the entire lawn in one efficient process. It was the sort of project a writer could handle while simultaneously dreaming up the next chapter.

Miranda was highly impressed by what she saw. Her ex had once declared he would rather find himself in a casket than at the controls of a lawn mower. He had grown up in a wealthy family whose members abstained from getting their hands dirty, and that mindset had followed him into a brief and unhappy marriage. His aversion to yard work had always seemed somehow un-American to her but never more than now as she watched Grant speed across the yard, dutifully executing one of his house-sitting chores. There was a certain nobility in this sort of simple work that she found appealing.

When Grant saw her, he smiled, waved, and veered off course, instantly churning a dozen trumpet daffodils into a silky powder that covered the lawn like lemony snow. He was momentarily horrified, but Miranda, pretending not to notice, knew the evidence would be long gone by the time Naomi returned from Israel. A year from now the daffodils would be as good as new.

"You look like a pro up there," she said as he turned off the engine and climbed down to greet her. "The lawn looks wonderful."

"I didn't screw up too badly, did I? Only a few minor problems."

"As long as Naomi's prize roses are intact, you're fine."

They sat on the patio in the late-morning sunshine, Grant wondering whether Miranda had read his latest effort and Miranda wondering how to break the bad news. After an uncomfortable silence, Grant spoke first.

"Since you're not telling me how great the new version is, can I assume you didn't like it?"

"It's vastly better than that *thing* you shared a few days ago," she said, making a face, "but it's not nearly as good as you're capable of. Remember, I read your short stories and thought they were excellent. This doesn't compare."

"The plot isn't all that original, I guess."

"When it comes to love stories, there's really nothing new under the sun. The plots are always comfortably familiar, and readers expect that. It's the characters who reside within your plot that need work."

Her critique was detailed, comprehensive, and positive. The characters in his short stories, she told him, were three-dimensional and highly believable. She knew what they looked like, what they thought, and what they felt as they experienced their triumphs and failures. But the characters in this latest draft were overly flat and one-dimensional, more shadows of people than people.

"You need to breathe life into them," she said. "I see names and faces, but I don't feel anything about the characters, and *feeling* is the essence of romance. The characters need to be likable or detestable, charming or disagreeable, honest or dishonest, bold or timid. That sort of thing."

He stared into the distance as he quietly considered Miranda's comments. This was unfamiliar territory for him. After all, he's the one who had been lecturing students on the fundamentals of fiction writing, and character development had always been a core issue. Why had he failed to follow his own advice?

"You're right," he finally said. "My short stories were largely autobiographical, and the characters were essentially versions of people I actually knew and understood. I guess that's another way of saying I don't really know what the heck I'm talking about when it comes to romance." He hesitated a moment before adding, "Maybe this whole idea is a mistake."

Miranda disagreed. "You don't need to murder people in order to write convincing murder mysteries, and you don't need to have your heart broken in order to write convincingly about heartbreak. You do, however, need to immerse yourself in the romance genre. How many Hallmark movies have you watched since I last saw you?"

"He pretended to count on his fingers. "Uh, none. I saw some really good baseball games, though."

"Ah, so you want to be a sportswriter?"

"Okay, point taken. Tonight I'll watch a Hallmark movie."

"That's a beginning."

"Do you want to watch it with me?"

"I can't," she said. "I'm having dinner with a college friend who's in town. But I'm counting on you to watch a movie, not another baseball game."

He gave her a thumbs-up. "Where are you going for dinner?"

"Les Bois. My friend and I both love French food, and we're not interested in driving to Manhattan."

"Smart move." When she got up to leave, he said, "Do you want a bottle of water or something?"

"No, thanks. I have a hair appointment before dinner. Rain check on the water?"

"Of course." He walked her to her car. "I'll call you tomorrow and tell you how the movie was."

"I'll be there."

He waved as she drove off, but she didn't notice. She was already talking on the phone with someone.

29.

Grant sat down at 7:00 that night for the same meal he prepared at least three times each week: tuna salad on multigrain bread, Annie's organic mac and cheese, and a small can of Bush's baked beans. He paused after every few bites to toss scraps of the sandwich and bits of macaroni to Rajah, who over the past several days had begun begging for handouts from atop the kitchen table rather than from the floor. The new arrangement didn't bother Grant in the least, but he assumed he might have to break Rajah of the habit before Naomi returned.

After dinner he carried his dishes to the sink while the cat licked the table clean, another routine that would probably need to be modified at some point in the coming months. Until then, the team effort made perfect sense. It saved Grant from having to wipe the table down, and it guaranteed that no food would ever go to waste.

Grant now faced his major decision of the evening. An outstanding baseball game and a Hallmark movie both began at 8:00, which meant one of them had to be recorded. Since he had promised Miranda he would watch the movie, he thought that's what he should do first. On the other hand, the game was live, and he wasn't sold on the idea of watching a recorded version. But what if he watched the game first and it went into extra innings? In that case he might not begin watching the movie until after midnight and would run the risk of falling asleep during it. If that happened, he would not be able to tell Miranda he had, in fact, watched the thing. In the end, his promise to Miranda carried the vote. He would watch the Hallmark movie and then fast-forward through the baseball game before going to bed.

The movie was hardly the sort of thing he would have chosen if left to his own devices. No one was kidnapped, no missiles were fired, and dozens of enemy combatants didn't die. But he found the story surprisingly agreeable nevertheless. A pretty young woman vacationed in a small New England town and met a handsome young fireman who loved puppies. Two minutes after the movie began, he knew with absolute certainty where this was going. Sure enough, after a series of humorous coincidences, charming false starts, and innocent misunderstandings, the pretty young woman and the handsome young fireman fell in love. At the very end of the movie they shared a pure, G-rated kiss and presumably lived happily ever after.

What Grant found most instructive about the movie was the extent to which he was invited inside the heads of the two main characters. They spoke freely with each other and with their friends about the infinite complexity of life. Love, fear, joy, decency, and hope were all given their turn under the microscope, and it didn't take long for Grant to understand why the characters were motivated to do the things they did. They were fully formed, three-dimensional characters whose behavior evolved naturally from what they thought and said.

Three strange things happened as soon as the movie ended. First, Grant automatically picked up the phone to call Miranda, then put it back on the coffee table when he remembered she was having dinner at Les Bois. Second, he discovered he was no longer in the mood to watch a baseball game, though he didn't know why. Third, and strangest of all, he found himself trying to remember whether the friend Miranda was having dinner with was male or female.

After thinking back on their conversation, he realized that, whether deliberately or not, she had been vague about her "college friend" who, like her, loved French food. Then he also remembered she said she was going to have her hair done after leaving Naomi's. Finally, he pictured himself waving goodbye to her as drove away. She didn't wave back because she was already on the phone.

It all added up. There was undoubtedly another man in her life. And as the pain of that recognition set in, he reluctantly admitted to himself that Miranda had inadvertently become much more than a friend.

He sat in front of the TV until shortly after midnight, aimlessly flipping channels in a futile effort to keep his mind off Miranda and her so-called friend. He imagined them gazing across the table at each other in the flickering candlelight, whispering suggestively in flawless French. The man, ruggedly handsome and debonair, poured more champagne and told her he loved what she had done with her hair. She took the compliment in stride, not bothering to mention that a few hours earlier she had paid a stylist one hundred dollars to coif the hair just for him.

Over dessert he asked her to spend a few weeks with him at his six-million-dollar apartment overlooking the Jardin du Luxembourg in Paris. They would stay at her place tonight, he said, and in the morning drive to Teterboro Airport in his Ferrari and then board his Gulfstream G500 for the flight to Paris-Le Bourget Airport. She could pack light because he would take her shopping along the Avenue des Champs-Élysées and outfit her in the latest fashions. One of the stops, naturally, would be Etam, for lingerie. She might want to pick out an enticing silk camisole suitable for lounging on the balcony in the evening and perhaps a black Brazilian bikini in case they jetted to Biarritz for a few days at the beach.

What little sleep Grant got that night was troubled by images of Miranda and her wealthy boyfriend frolicking through Europe without a care in the world.

And always in the background he heard his sister's voice: *Miranda's the one, little brother. Don't blow it.*

30.

Rajah pounced on the bed at 6:30 a.m., declaring it was time for breakfast. Usually Grant ignored him until the growling began three or four minutes later, but this time he rose immediately and stumbled toward the kitchen, bleary-eyed and exhausted, because he had already been awake for nearly two hours. He didn't breathe as he spooned the liver-and-chicken goo into Rajah's dish, then escaped to the living room as fast as he could.

He flopped on the couch and for the thousandth time asked himself why he had been so slow to recognize his feelings toward Miranda. Shouldn't his sister's urgent warning have been enough to get him moving? Yes, it should have, but he had persisted in ignoring the obvious and now feared he would never recover from the damage he had done.

He could try, though. He decided he would call Miranda at 8:00. If she was alone rather than in her lover's arms, he would ask to see her. If she said yes, he would know he still had a chance. If she said no, well, he had no idea what he would do. He might not know until the moment arrived.

The small brass clock on the end table said it was 6:38, and he began to wonder whether he really had to wait until 8:00. Maybe 7:00 wouldn't be too early. Then he grew upset with himself for not even knowing what time she normally got up in the morning. It was the sort of thing a man should know about a woman who mattered to him, but he had never gotten around to learning even the most basic things about her life. Instead, he had been content to be on the receiving end of her friendship and sound advice. She had given, and he had taken. It was as simple as that. No wonder she had turned to someone else.

The clock's minute hand seemed almost frozen as it moved reluctantly toward 7:00. Finally, at 6:53, he could wait no longer. He called her landline rather than her cell phone because he wanted to be sure she was home, not at her lover's house or in a fancy hotel room, and his chest tightened when the phone began to ring. He hoped to sound casual even though he realized the next few minutes might change the course of his life, but his resolve vanished when the recorded message cut in after the fifth ring: *This is Miranda. I can't take your call right now, so please leave a message.*

"Hi, it's me," he said nervously. "I hope I'm not calling too early. When you get a chance, please give me a call."

He filled the next hour by caring for Naomi's indoor jungle, brushing Rajah, and taking a quick shower. Then at 8:00 he called Miranda's landline again, this time hanging up after the fourth ring. At this point he knew that one of two things was true. Either she was there and unwilling to take his calls, or she had spent the night elsewhere with her "friend." And, yes, she might even be on her way to France with her secret lover. Anything was possible.

When she hadn't called by 9:00, he decided to take a walk. He had simply been out getting some exercise, he would tell her, and decided to stop by and say hello when he passed her house. If she invited him in, he could look for signs that another man had been there. Two wine glasses in the sink, perhaps—one with lipstick on the rim, one without. If, on the other hand, she kept him at the partially opened front door, afraid of who or what he might find inside, he would know that his sister's worst fear had come to pass. He had blown it.

At 9:20 he rang her doorbell and waited for what seemed an eternity. He peered through one of the sidelights and thought he saw movement in the kitchen. It might have been the shadow of a backyard tree swaying in the morning breeze, or it might have been Miranda hiding from him behind the refrigerator. He rang the bell again, rapped three times on the door, and finally walked away. Then noticed that the shade on the garage window had been pulled down, making it impossible for him to know whether her car was inside. Was the shade always down, or had she pulled it down this morning after his first phone call, one more sign that his presence was no longer welcome? He was afraid to guess.

He was halfway to Naomi's when the BMW pulled up alongside him and through the open passenger-side window Miranda said, "Perfect morning for a walk. Want some company?"

Grant's face lit up. "Absolutely."

"Climb in. I'll park at your place." She waited for him to fasten his seat belt, then said, "I just got back from taking Lydia to Westchester County Airport. She had a 7:30 flight to D.C."

"Who's Lydia?"

"The college friend I told you I was having dinner with last night. I hadn't seen her for two years, and we had a great time."

"How was dinner?"

"Fabulous. I had the duck à l'orange."

"That's what you had when you and I went there," Grant said, surprising himself more than Miranda. It wasn't the sort of thing he usually remembered.

"Exactly. And it was out of this world. Then we went back to my place and talked until midnight."

She parked in Naomi's driveway, and they began to walk. It was a stunning spring day with bright sunshine and the temperature headed toward eighty-five. Miranda spared him the details of her long conversation with Lydia, including her friend's speculation about Grant.

"This guy sounds more than simply clueless, Miranda," she had said. *"I think he's either gay or asexual. What do you see in him?"*

"Among other things, he's kind, smart, and attractive."

"Puppies are also kind, smart, and attractive, Miranda, and they're a lot easier to train."

"Does Lydia live in D.C.?"

"She works for the State Department, so she travels a lot. I probably won't see her for a year or so. So what did you do last night?"

"I watched my first Hallmark movie," he said proudly. "I called you this morning to tell you, but you were already on your way to the airport. That was around 7:00, which was probably too early to call."

"Not at all. I'm up every day by 6:00," she said, "and I work out for thirty or forty minutes. So tell me about the movie."

What followed was a lengthy and insightful critique of the plot, the characters, and the acting, all of which got high passing marks. It was clear to him that Marcy Yum's trashy novel represented one end of the romance spectrum and that Hallmark represented the other. Also clear was which direction his own novel should move in.

"I think a little more physical contact between the two main characters would have made the story seem more real-world," he noted, "but basically I liked it a lot."

"Romance novels generally have more sex in them than you'll find in Hallmark movies, but there's no need to get carried away."

"As I did in my first attempt."

She nodded. "As you did in your first attempt."

"The characters in the movie were also believable and much more complex than the characters in my second attempt."

"It's easier with a movie," she noted, "because you see the characters in action. You see their facial expressions and how they interact with each other. But when you read a novel, you have to rely on the author to supply all the information you can't see. Too much information causes the story to bog down. But too little leaves the characters flat and unbelievable."

They strolled slowly through the community park, a ninety-acre oasis of tall trees, shady walks, and vast stretches of daffodils that had been growing there for decades. A duck family paddled serenely across the pond at the center of the park while two small children and their mother stood along the bank, hoping the ducks would join them.

"I think I need to do more research before writing again," Grant said.

"I'm glad you think so because I have an idea. Actually, it's Dana's idea."

Dana had suggested that Miranda and Grant spend a few days at the vacation home she and Jim had purchased several years earlier at Lake George. The waterfront home offered magnificent scenery as well as complete seclusion. It sounded ideal, Miranda said, for reading, watching a few more movies, and perhaps working on the outline of a novel.

Grant was attracted to the idea until he thought about Naomi's three-ring binder.

"I've got Rajah, the indoor flowers, the outdoor shrubs, the lawn . . ."

"Whenever Naomi goes away for a few days, her neighbor Karen takes care of everything except the lawn, which you can mow before we leave."

"She knows how to take care of Rajah?"

"Yes, she and Rajah are old friends."

"Are you sure Naomi would be okay with the idea?"

"Positive. I texted her two days ago, and she thought we should go to Lake George before Jim and Dana settle in for the summer."

"Then I guess we should." He thought for a moment, turned to her, and stopped walking. "I really missed you last night," he said softly.

She moved closer and said, "I'm glad."

Their long first kiss left no doubt in Grant's mind that he had been a fool for dragging his feet.

31.

As Grant and Miranda were walking out of the park, Hickston College's vice president for financial affairs, Ezra Goodman, was walking into the president's office alongside a trim thirtyish man in a dark blue suit. They looked like a matched set of angry Dobermans.

Farnsworth wasn't much happier. He was supposed to have left the campus ten minutes earlier to play a round of golf with the CEO of a local company, but his secretary had told him that Goodman was on his way to discuss an urgent and extremely confidential matter that could not wait.

"This better be good, Ezra," Farnsworth snapped, "because I'm supposed to be on my way to an important meeting."

"It's not good at all, Porter," Goodman said bluntly. "This is FBI Special Agent Jorge Suarez. He's a criminal enterprise specialist."

The words *criminal enterprise* had a numbing effect on Farnsworth, and he warily extended his hand to the FBI agent.

"You should probably sit down for this," Suarez suggested.

After waiting for Farnsworth to take the agent's advice, Goodman laid out the grim facts as succinctly as possible. Over the past several days, someone with access to Hickston's bank accounts had initiated a series of fraudulent wire transfers totaling slightly more than two million dollars. The theft was discovered only when a vendor called to complain that one of Hickston's checks had bounced.

"That call came just before 5:00 p.m. yesterday," Goodman explained. "The staff member who spoke with the vendor assumed it was a simple clerical error at the bank, and she said she would take care of it first thing in the morning. But after digging around this morning, she learned that all of our cash holdings have vanished from three different banks. I contacted the FBI, and Agent Suarez drove right up from the White Plains office."

When Farnsworth was finally able to find his voice, he asked the obvious question. "How could that much money leave the banks without our permission?"

Suarez answered in a crisp monotone. "Number one, the criminals who perpetrate crimes like this are smarter, better trained, and more highly motivated than bank employees. Number two, the transfers were authorized properly from inside Hickston's computer system, which means the bank had no reason to question the transactions."

"Are you telling me a Hickston employee stole the money?" Farnsworth asked, his outrage growing.

Suarez nodded. "That's how it looks."

"Do you know who?"

Referring to the small notebook in his left hand, Suarez said, "Someone named Hannah Grackle, whereabouts unknown."

While the situation was growing increasingly tense on the Hickston campus, Grackle was sipping a mimosa on the balcony of her two-bedroom suite at the luxurious Hamilton Princess in Bermuda. She had flown in two days earlier to spend a week of uninterrupted bliss with her paramour, James Corcoran, the man she had brought to Farnsworth's year-end reception. Unfortunately, for the past forty-eight hours Corcoran, a billionaire hedge fund manager from Miami, had been unexpectedly delayed by an especially complex business transaction. In the meantime, he had told her, she should relax, do some shopping, and dine like royalty in the hotel's several restaurants. All charges, including nearly four thousand dollars per night for the suite, would go straight to his credit card.

Corcoran promised he would apologize properly in person when he arrived. He was especially fond of a particular jewelry store on Front Street, he said, hinting that he would buy something with a large diamond for her ring finger. Having spent his life searching for the right woman, he was finally ready to turn the reins of his business over to someone else and devote himself to love.

Grackle was more than ready. She had once sworn off marriage, believing that her research and publishing were far more worthwhile pursuits than tending to a man, a house, and a dog. But Corcoran had changed her mind in only eight days. They had met in Steinville one fateful afternoon while he was in town secretly finalizing the purchase of a software firm. After dining that same evening at MacArthur's in West Point, they had been inseparable until he had been forced to fly back to Miami and run his investment firm. Before leaving, however, he had booked the opulent suite at the Hamilton Princess and told her that perhaps they would jet to Italy after sampling the best that Bermuda had to offer. He had devoted his life to making money. Now he wanted to spend it.

Gazing out upon the shimmering waters of Hamilton Bay, she admitted to herself that Corcoran was hardly an ideal catch. Although he seemed to know a great deal about investing, he was wholly untutored when it came to things like literature, art, and history. Beyond that, he was by no means what she could call handsome, or even modestly attractive. He was short, squat, badly out of shape, and, yes, rather ugly. But he could be a brilliant conversationalist when the right topic came along, and he had been eloquent in telling her why he found himself unbearably attracted to her. He said that he loved her intelligence, strength, and honesty, and during an especially torrid scene in her bedroom he had proclaimed her a sex goddess sent to him from above. Although he was quick to add that sex was the lesser part of what she meant to him, she found the praise both surprising and more than a little stimulating. She had never thought of herself as a sex goddess, but she was willing to get used to the idea.

All she needed now was for James Corcoran to join the pre-wedding festivities.

32.

At 9:00 the next morning Grant picked Miranda up for the drive to Lake George, and at 1:15, after stopping along the way for an early lunch, they pulled into the long gravel driveway that snaked its way through the woods to Jim and Dana's lakefront vacation home. Dana had casually referred to it as a cottage, but her description hardly did the place justice. A quick tour of the interior revealed that the two-story, four-thousand-foot structure held five bedrooms, four baths, high-end architectural details throughout, and, perhaps best of all, a covered porch that ran the entire length of the house and offered unobstructed views of the lake.

The home was nestled serenely in the midst of dense woods filled with mountain laurel. Jim and Dana apparently valued their privacy because the only other homes visible from their property were those located far across the lake. A wide front lawn sloped down to a private beach, where a metal rack held two canoes. In the middle of the lawn a pair of green Adirondack chairs sat alongside a flower garden in full bloom.

"How can a college professor afford something like this?" Grant wondered aloud as he admired the scene.

"I suspect it's because Dana is an advertising executive."

"Ah, of course. Did she say how often they use the place?"

"A week at a time now and then, but mostly weekends. It's a pretty easy drive."

"Especially in Naomi's S-Class." He grinned and said, "I may have to buy one of those with my first million."

"Why not write your first novel before you decide how to spend the first million?"

"You're probably right."

They left their suitcases in the foyer and settled into the Adirondack chairs to soak up some afternoon sunshine while talking seriously about the work ahead of them. To Grant's dismay, Miranda had brought with her a list of movies that she considered required viewing for someone about to launch a career as a romance writer. The list included *Casablanca, An Affair to Remember, Doctor Zhivago, Notting Hill, Beauty and the Beast, Love Story, The Sound of Music, Sleepless in Seattle, Shakespeare in Love,* and *West Side Story.* She wasn't at all surprised to learn that Grant had never seen any of them.

"All the movies are available on cable," she was happy to report, "and Dana insists on covering the rental fees as a getaway present for you and me."

"That sounds like a lot of hours in front of a television," Grant said disconsolately. "Do you think we'll ever have time to take one of the canoes out?"

"We'll go canoeing as often as you'd like. If we watch two movies each day, we'll still have about twenty hours a day left over to do anything we want."

"Did I count ten movies on the list?"

"You did."

"So you're thinking we'll be here for five days?"

"Why not? Rajah and Naomi's home are in good hands, and I'm convinced that investing your time in these movies will jump-start your writing."

He grinned. "Did you bring any popcorn?"

"No popcorn. Also no peanuts or Cracker Jack. This isn't a baseball game, Grant. It's work."

"In that case," he said, gamely throwing in the towel, "we'd better get started."

Once inside the house, Miranda suggested watching a movie before unpacking the suitcases, and Grant was fine with that. He was the willing student and she was the eager teacher. The first movie she cued up was *Sleepless in Seattle* starring Tom Hanks and Meg Ryan.

"This is a great way to begin," she said, "because it's funny and light-hearted even though the central story is quite moving."

And with that, the education of Grant Hunter, aspiring romance novelist, began. They sat quietly alongside each other on the comfortable down-filled sofa and watched as Annie Reed searched for the love of her life at the same time widower Sam Baldwin was abandoning the idea of ever falling in love again. All hope seemed lost when, almost magically, Annie and Sam met atop the Empire State Building and walked hand in hand into their happy future.

It was an ending that always left Miranda a mess. As usual, she began crying before the final scene actually began, and she had to stifle a sob when Annie and Sam first laid eyes on each other at the Empire State Building. She dabbed her eyes with a tissue and looked over at Grant, thinking there was a strong possibility he would be laughing at her for getting so emotional over a movie.

To her enormous shock, she saw tears rolling down his cheeks.

He shrugged and said, "Kind of sappy, huh?"

"The movie?"

"No, me."

"I don't think it's sappy at all. I think it's nice."

"Are all the other movies like that?"

"Some are happy, some are sad, but all of them are wildly romantic."

He wiped away his tears. "I hope I survive."

"I'm confident you will." She paused for a moment. "Want to take the suitcases upstairs now?"

"Sure."

He carried both suitcases and stopped at the door of the first bedroom he came to. It was a small but inviting room, its view of the lake partially obscured by a towering pine.

"Want me to take this one?" he asked.

She shook her head and motioned for him to follow her down the hall to the sunlit master suite at the corner. The room offered stunning views of the lake on one side and the forest on the other, and it had a small balcony ideal for coffee in the morning or sunsets in the evening. The centerpiece was a king bed topped with a handmade floral quilt that was worth considerably more than Grant's old Hyundai. Across the room from the bed was a gas fireplace with a large flat-screen TV mounted on the wall above it.

"You can leave both suitcases here," she said. "I want to show you something." She led him to the master bath, which featured a large jetted tub with more than enough room for two. "Dana said it's extremely relaxing. Want to find out?"

He did.

Two hours later, having tested both the tub and the king bed, they agreed that their Lake George getaway held incredible promise. Though the next few days would require immense stamina, they believed themselves equal to the challenge.

33.

Grackle was four days into her lavish but lonely stay at the Hamilton Princess, still waiting for the elusive James Corcoran, CEO of Excelse Global Investments, Inc., to make his first appearance. He had called her the evening before her flight to Bermuda and explained that he was in the final stages of closing the most important deal of his career. He would be unreachable for the next day or two, he said, but the instant he signed the papers, he would be on the way to her loving arms.

She was frustrated by his lateness, of course, but she made the best of the situation by falling into a pleasant routine. A white-jacketed room service attendant served her breakfast on the balcony each morning. After that she lounged poolside until the sun grew too strong for her sensitive skin. Then she changed and did some shopping, constantly charging resort wear, jewelry, and souvenirs to her room. She ate lunch and dinner at the hotel's restaurants and liberally sampled the extensive wine list. She grew fond of fresh seafood stew and pan-seared snapper, and she decided that Veuve Clicquot champagne, at thirty dollars per glass, went well with almost anything, including molten chocolate cake.

There were only two things she did not do during her time alone. First, she declined to step on the bathroom scale. She could tell she was rapidly gaining weight, but she felt confident she would lose it once she and Corcoran began mauling each other after their long separation. Second, she refused to check voice messages on her home phone because there was no one she wanted to hear from, especially not while living the good life in Bermuda. One of the voice messages she therefore did not hear was from American Express.

"*We believe your credit card may have been stolen,*" the polite customer service rep said, "*because someone has been using it for purchases in Bermuda, and your credit limit has been exceeded.*"

Unaware of the mounting financial crisis, she was blissfully drinking a second mojito poolside at 11:00 a.m. as things were rapidly heading south for her back at Hickston College. An octogenarian campus security officer unlocked the door to her office for FBI Special Agent Jorge Suarez, who had been joined by a colleague, Special Agent Marla Kincaid, a cybercrime specialist. Suarez promised to lock up when he and Kincaid were finished, and the bald old man in the rumpled uniform left them to their investigation.

It took Kincaid less than a minute to get inside Grackle's desktop computer and begin exploring its contents. For the next two hours she and Suarez examined files related to department policies, lesson plans, student grades, and other mind-numbing topics that had nothing to do with financial matters. At that point they began searching through her emails, and that's when Kincaid spotted the red flag. Two weeks earlier, Grackle had received an email from James Corcoran asking her to install an app that would allow them to email each other through his company's heavily encrypted network. Given the highly sensitive nature of his work, he had explained, it was vital for him to use this method of communicating, even with the woman he adored.

The app had instantly infected her computer and opened the door to a secure Hickston system that was normally accessible only to senior administrators and faculty chairpersons like Grackle. In the right hands, the system could readily unlock the college's bank accounts.

"The app she downloaded is one I've seen before," Kincaid told Suarez. "It was developed by the Russian mafia for ransomware attacks on large corporations, and it can easily be modified to gain control of a firm's financial system. Obviously, that's what happened in this case."

"Do you think she was in on the scheme?"

"Probably. I assume she told him to bury the app in an email so that she could later claim she didn't know what she was doing."

"Makes sense. So how does a guy named James Corcoran get access to an app used by Russian hackers?"

"Wild guess? His name isn't James Corcoran. But we can do some checking."

The first step in checking Corcoran's credentials didn't take long. Kincaid's cybercrime unit in Washington quickly verified that Excelse

Global Investments was nothing more than a dummy website built to dupe gullible people like Hannah Grackle.

The next step in the process took three hours but was also successful. After obtaining a photo of Corcoran and Grackle taken at Farnsworth's recent outdoor reception, Suarez emailed the image to the FBI's Facial Analysis, Comparison, and Evaluation (FACE) Services unit. Using the most sophisticated facial-recognition software available and then accessing a host of government databases, the FACE team determined that "James Corcoran" was in truth Oleg Gruzdev, a Russian mafia minor-leaguer who had fled his country after running afoul of a particularly nasty crime boss. Grackle was either his victim or his willing accomplice. Time alone would tell.

Suarez and Kincaid walked across campus to the administration building and pulled the president from an emergency session of the board of trustees. Farnsworth was delighted to leave the boardroom since the meeting was going even worse than he had expected. The board had been grilling him and his financial vice president for most of the day, seeking to determine which of them should be fired over the two-million-dollar theft. At the moment, the finger seemed to be pointing at him.

Farnsworth listened in disbelief as Kincaid walked him through the basics of how Hickston's money had disappeared. By downloading the Russian malware sent to her by Oleg Gruzdev, aka James Corcoran, Grackle had given him unfettered access to the college's computer network. Once inside, he breached the firewall that normally kept the school's financial-management system separate from all other campus activities. At that point he could use either his laptop or his cell phone to move money at will.

"He tested his capabilities with several relatively small transactions," Kincaid said, "all of which went smoothly. Satisfied with the results, he then wired all the cash from your three banks to Grackle's account in Switzerland. The money sat there briefly before being wired to three separate accounts in the Cayman Islands, Belize, and Singapore. Finally, all the money was wired to Nevis, and that's where the trail ends."

"Why in God's name would the trail end?" Farnsworth sputtered.

"Because Nevis banks don't cooperate with outsiders," Suarez said. "Maybe the money is still there, but maybe it's long gone. We'll never know."

"So what do I tell the board of trustees? Are the banks responsible for covering the losses?"

Suarez shook his head. "Highly unlikely. If the banks followed all the procedures that they and the college agreed to when the accounts were first established, you're out of luck."

While Farnsworth was with Suarez and Kincaid attempting to digest the grim news, Vice President Ezra Goodman was frantically spilling his guts to the board in a valiant effort to save his own skin. Among other things, he produced a memo he had sent to Farnsworth three years earlier recommending that the college strengthen its accounting-and-finance system.

"I told Porter it was a huge mistake to have our antiquated financial system linked in any way to the main campus computer network, but he refused to spend eighty thousand dollars on the project."

"Why did he think the new financial system wasn't necessary?" asked Herman Withers, the board's chairman.

"He told me we had more important uses for the money. Then a few weeks later," Goodman quickly added, "he had me pay ninety thousand dollars for a new Cadillac Escalade to replace his one-year-old Cadillac sedan. I can't say for sure that the new financial system would have prevented this theft, but it certainly would have done more for us than the new Cadillac."

Goodman was dismissed from the meeting, and on his way down the hall he bumped into Farnsworth, who had bid the two FBI agents farewell.

"How's it going in there?" Farnsworth asked nervously.

"Quite well," Goodman lied. "I think you're in good shape."

The smile Farnsworth wore as he entered the boardroom disappeared as soon as the chairman asked, "Why did you choose to buy a Cadillac Escalade instead of upgrading the school's deficient accounting-and-finance system?"

"I think you're comparing apples and oranges," Farnsworth blustered. "The new finance system was a frivolous expense because we already had a system that worked just fine. The new vehicle, on the other hand, was a necessary fundraising investment. When I go out to visit wealthy donors and foundations, I need to represent a thriving and prosperous college." He thought for a moment, then added indignantly, "You can't expect me to do that in a Ford Fiesta."

Then the questioning took a dangerous turn for the beleaguered president.

"Tell us what the FBI agents had to say," Withers demanded.

So Farnsworth did. By the end of his sorry tale, everyone in the room knew that his failure to upgrade Hickston's finance system had ended up costing the college two million dollars. He was asked to step out of the room while the board members weighed the available evidence.

When he was invited back inside five minutes later, he was informed that a special board committee would be on campus for the next week or two conducting a full investigation of Hickston's management policies and procedures.

Withers made it unmistakably clear that Farnsworth's continued employment was hanging in the balance.

34.

Grant and Miranda began their fourth day at Lake George by taking one of the canoes out just after sunrise, when mist was on the water and the resident loons were calling plaintively to each other. The whole world seemed at rest as they worked their way among the small islands just offshore from Jim and Dana's home.

Their paddling skills had improved radically since the first attempt, when they had managed to turn the canoe upside down shortly after leaving the beach. They were now a highly efficient team capable of matching each other's strokes and navigating even the trickiest obstacles. Canoeing had become pure fun instead of hard work.

Their progress as canoeists was outmatched only by their progress as lovers. The fresh Adirondack air and a steady diet of romantic movies had conspired to topple Grant's few remaining inhibitions, and he knew there would be no turning back. They were meant to be a couple.

"Want to just drift for a while?" he asked.

She stopped paddling. "What a perfect morning."

The canoe's momentum carried them closer to an island where a great blue heron waded the shallows in search of breakfast. Sunlight filtered through the island's tall spruces, creating a rainbow quilt on the wavelets, as Grant and Miranda shared the feeling of floating away from the rest of the world.

After a brief hesitation, Grant told her what he had never told anyone before.

"I love you, Miranda."

She turned to him, smiled, and said, "I love you, too, Grant. But I won't try to hug you right now."

"Good idea. The water is kind of deep here."

The embrace and the long kiss that went with it waited until they returned to Jim and Dana's. The day had scarcely begun, but Grant had already taken a quantum leap toward becoming a romance writer.

After storing the canoe, they ate a light breakfast of scrambled eggs, toast, and coffee on the back patio. They were nearly finished when Miranda announced that the day's curriculum would be the most challenging yet. They would be watching two movies with a combined run time of more than six hours: *Doctor Zhivago* and *The Sound of Music*.

"One of them is about pain, suffering, and the torture that love can bring," she told him. "The other is happy, triumphant, and uplifting. Which do you want to watch first?"

"Let's get the pain and suffering out of the way and finish with something happy."

"Excellent choice. Class begins as soon as you get another cup of coffee."

They watched *Doctor Zhivago*, took a quick lunch break, then watched *The Sound of Music*. In the first movie, which lasted three hours and seventeen minutes, handsome young Dr. Yuri Zhivago fell in love with the beautiful Lara Antipova, endured a lifetime of unimaginable hardship, and was finally crushed by the forces of evil. In the second movie, which ran for two hours and fifty-four minutes, an exuberant young novitiate named Maria left her convent, fell in love with a retired naval captain, and lived happily ever after.

Both movies left them in tears.

"So, what do you think?" Miranda asked when Maria and her new family finally walked off the screen while a choir sang "Climb Every Mountain."

"*Doctor Zhivago* was a gorgeous movie to watch, but I don't like sad endings. *The Sound of Music* is much more my thing."

"Mine as well, but both endings reflect the real world. If you're going to write romance, you have to embrace all the possibilities."

"But don't readers prefer a happy ending?"

"I'm sure they do, but a mixture of sadness and happiness helps keep a story interesting and stands a better chance of connecting with your readers."

She thought for a moment. "Romance readers want you to take them on an emotional roller coaster ride. Giving them a taste of defeat along the way allows them to appreciate victory all the more."

"As in *The Sound of Music.*"

"Exactly. Maria's path to happiness was filled with challenge and sometimes failure. That's what makes the happy ending so much more satisfying."

Grant nodded and appeared ready to continue the discussion but changed his mind after glancing at his watch.

"You have a date?" she asked playfully.

"Not a date, but something I need to do in town."

"Want me to come with you?"

He shook his head. "I won't be long."

After a lingering kiss that nearly made him change his mind about leaving, Grant drove off, promising to be back within an hour or so. The first thing Miranda did when she was alone was call Dana to offer a progress report.

Dana answered on the first ring. "Is all well at Lake George?" she asked.

"Much better than well. Grant has earned a perfect grade in all aspects of his romance education."

"*All* aspects?"

"Yes, *all.* In fact, I'm hoping we haven't worn out your mattress."

"Not to worry. It came with a ten-year warranty, so feel free to demand the most from your student. Where is he, by the way?"

"He went into town but wouldn't say why. It's a secret mission."

"I love secrets."

"So do I as long as they're pleasant."

"Actually, I have one *unpleasant* surprise to share if you have a minute."

According to Dana, Jim had heard through the grapevine that someone had broken into Hickston's bank accounts and stolen all the available cash. Farnsworth was apparently very much under the gun, as one would expect, but there was also an unconfirmed rumor that Grackle was somehow involved in the theft. That part was highly speculative, Dana noted, but it was intriguing nevertheless. Like most people, she found Grackle loathsome.

"I can easily imagine Hannah kicking a puppy, but for some reason I can't picture her as a bank robber."

"Well, as I said, that part of the story is just a rumor so far. Maybe the facts will come out by the time you and Grant return to Steinville. But don't be in a hurry to get here," she added hastily, "because Jim and I won't be driving up to the lake for another two weeks."

"Thanks for the kind offer, but I think we'll be leaving tomorrow. Grant feels guilty about not taking care of Naomi's home and cat while we're up here. I told him everything's fine, but . . ."

"But he's conscientious."

"He absolutely is, Dana, and he's also turning out to be the most thoughtful man I've ever met."

"*Thoughtful man*," she laughed. "Now those are two words you rarely find in the same sentence."

"I agree completely. Yet here we are."

"And you're happy."

"Incredibly happy, yes. And I owe that to you for letting us stay here."

"It would have happened one way or the other," Dana insisted, "but maybe the lake house accelerated the process. If so, I'm glad."

Grant returned an hour and a half later, apologized for having taken so long, and placed two large paper bags on the kitchen island.

"I want to make a special dinner on our last night here," he said, "but I don't normally do a lot of shopping, so this took longer than expected." From the first bag he removed two prime rib eyes for the grill as well as two baking potatoes and a head of broccoli for roasting. "I've never roasted broccoli before, but the woman at the store said it's easy."

"It's very easy," she assured him. "I'll show you how."

"I've also never baked a potato. Well, not one that was actually fully baked, I mean."

"I can manage the potatoes."

The last item from the first bag was a small white candle.

"I assume there's a candle holder somewhere in the house," he said hopefully. "I thought dinner by candlelight on the balcony would be nice."

She leaned over and kissed him lightly on the cheek.

"That would be lovely," she said.

From the second bag he took a bottle of Moët & Chandon champagne. That earned him a kiss on the other cheek.

"Oh, there's one other thing in the car. I'll be right back."

He returned a few minutes later and handed her a clear vase that held a dozen red roses.

"For the best teacher ever," he said.

"They're beautiful, Grant. But I warned you about spending your first million before publishing your first book."

"No problem. When we get back to Steinville, Rajah will gladly share some of his canned food."

She knew he was only half-joking. His budget was tight and he was months, perhaps even years, from being able to support himself as a novelist. Yet he had wanted their final night at Lake George to be special, thereby confirming what she had told Dana earlier. Grant was the most thoughtful man she had ever met.

Miranda could not have scripted a more romantic evening: excellent food, fine champagne, and a candlelit table for two on the balcony. For that reason she decided to save the story about Hickston and Grackle for the ride back home.

Tonight they had better things to do.

35.

Grackle had asked for breakfast to be delivered at 9:00 a.m. sharp, but someone began knocking on her door at 8:00, long before she had combed out her hair or applied a half pound of makeup. Already in a foul mood because Corcoran still had not arrived in Bermuda, she marched to the door in her plush hotel bathrobe fully prepared to send the waiter away with a tongue-lashing.

But the two unsmiling men she found standing in the hallway were not dressed in white room-service jackets nor were they bearing trays filled with fresh fruit, croissants, and coffee. They both wore dark suits, and their name tags identified them as the hotel's manager and his security director. The taller of the two, the manager, held a long hotel bill in his right hand.

"Good morning. Are you Ms. Grackle?" he asked, attempting to sound pleasant.

"Yes, I am. And that," she said curtly, pointing to the doorknob, "is the DO NOT DISTURB sign I put there last night."

"Yes, well, we have a rather unfortunate situation." He handed her the bill. "Your room charges now total twenty-three thousand dollars, and American Express has declined your credit card."

She glared at him and said, "The room charges are *not* on my credit card. Mr. James Corcoran made the reservation using his own credit card."

"Mr. Corcoran may have made the reservation, but it was your American Express card that was presented upon check-in."

"That was only for incidentals," she said indignantly.

"No, that was for *all* charges, Ms. Grackle. And American Express tells us that your charges exceed your credit limit by approximately twelve thousand dollars. So, unless you have another credit card, we have a problem."

"No, Mr. Corcoran has a problem. He made the reservation and told me he would be picking up all the charges."

The security director, a powerfully built man with a thick neck and broad shoulders, finally spoke.

"Mr. Corcoran used your credit card, not his, when making the reservation. So I'm afraid Mr. Corcoran isn't the person who will be arrested by our local police if the bill isn't paid," he growled. "Would you care to provide a second credit card?"

Chastened by the prospect of finishing her vacation in a Bermuda jail cell, she agreed to report to the front desk as soon as she had changed. That momentarily satisfied the manager and the security director, both of whom thanked her for her time and wished her a good day.

The first thing she did was phone Corcoran's private number, only to learn that it was no longer in service. Then she emailed him, but the email was returned a few seconds later marked UNDELIVERABLE. At that point she panicked and called the number on the back of her American Express card and was connected to the fraud department. The conversation didn't last long. As soon as she confirmed that she was, in fact, staying at the Hamilton Princess, the customer-service rep told her that she was responsible for all charges.

Her hands were shaking by the time she reached the front desk and handed over her Visa card. Fortunately, the transaction went through. But after settling the room bill, she learned that her Visa card was only six hundred dollars short of her spending limit. That was barely enough to cover the cost of a shuttle to the airport in Bermuda, a one-way ticket to Newark Liberty, and a taxi from Newark to Steinville. What little cash she had in her pocketbook might allow her to buy a hamburger or perhaps a bag of peanuts somewhere along the way.

As she walked to the elevator, she noticed the hotel's security director watching her from across the lobby. He nodded slightly and smiled, apparently pleased he would not have to call the police on a deadbeat guest.

She tried calling Corcoran again when she reached her room, hoping she had simply dialed a wrong number the first time, but the number was unquestionably out of service. That Corcoran had deliberately misled her was now painfully obvious. What was completely unclear, though, was why. She had no idea what he could have gained by having her travel to Bermuda and then sticking her with the obscene hotel bill.

She thought back on the time they had spent together. He had, of course, been extremely attentive—the first attentive man of her life, in fact—and they had enjoyed passionate moments together. Not long moments, she recalled, but satisfactory moments nevertheless. At the same time, though, there had always been something mildly off-putting about him. His table manners were deficient, as she learned when he accompanied her to Farnsworth's outdoor reception. He held his fork with a fist, as though trying to kill what was on his plate, rather than balancing it between his thumb and forefinger. He also seemed uncomfortable making eye contact with anyone, including her. At times he reminded her of a meerkat, nervously looking around as though fearful of being pounced upon by something with large teeth.

And then there were the questions, always the questions. How are things going for Hickston? How large is the endowment? Is the college good at paying its bills on time? What internet system do college employees use? He often sounded as though he were looking to buy a college, but she doubted that was the case. He was just overly interested in Hickston's affairs. She had once thought this reflected his feelings for her, but now she wasn't so sure. Perhaps there had been an ulterior motive all along.

As she crammed her suitcase with all the frivolous things she had bought for herself in Bermuda—the lace teddy no one would ever see, the floral-print sarong she would never have the courage to wear outside of Bermuda—she imagined stuffing Corcoran into an unmarked grave. Fantasizing over his premature death helped cushion the blow of her humiliation.

After spending five hours in the airport lounge at Bermuda's L.F. Wade International Airport and nearly two hours in the last row of a cramped United flight, she stepped off the plane to find a pair of blue-suited FBI agents waiting for her as she exited the jetway.

It was a wholly unexpected reception, but at least it would save her the cost of a cab ride to Steinville.

36.

Grant and Miranda left for Steinville after a relaxing breakfast and traveled the narrow two-lane road that gently wound its way through the deep woods on Lake George's eastern shore. Early in the three-hour drive Miranda shared the rumor that Hickston's bank accounts had been raided and that Grackle might be involved. Grant's response surprised her.

"She's certainly a liar, as I learned the hard way," he said calmly, "but she's not the sort of person who would rob banks. That part of the rumor can't be true."

"That's a remarkably charitable thing to say given what she did to you. You're a very kind person, Grant."

"How can I hold a grudge? If she hadn't trashed my career, I wouldn't have tried writing a romance novel. And if I hadn't tried writing a romance novel, I wouldn't have come to Lake George and fallen in love with you." He reached over and took her hand. "So everything worked out perfectly. Well, except for the writing part."

"The writing part comes next, and you'll be fabulous."

"Wish me luck."

"Luck won't have anything to do with it. You're an excellent writer, and you just earned an A+ in *Romance 101*. So your novel will be wonderful."

"I'd like to sign up for *Romance 102* as soon as the course is available."

"I'm sure that can be arranged."

They spent most of the ride home tossing around ideas for Grant's first romance novel, agreeing that something light, contemporary, and perhaps humorous would be the best fit. Since they both liked happy endings, they knew the story should be upbeat as well as uplifting.

They also agreed that when it comes to love stories, there is nothing new under the sun. Basically, the story never changes: two people meet, overcome a series of challenges, and fall in love. What would set Grant's romance novel apart from the thousands of others that had preceded it would be the likability of the characters he created and the uniqueness of the situations they faced.

"When you write," Miranda advised him, "think about people you know as well as the characters you liked most in the movies we just watched. Then put them together with new looks, new voices, and new situations. It's not rocket science, fortunately. Romance readers expect the same outcome every time. Give them that, and they'll be happy."

By the time he dropped her off at her house, he had what he believed was a workable storyline in his head, and he was eager to sit down and commit words to paper. But his feline housemate had other plans for him.

Rajah, it turned out, did not appreciate having been left in a neighbor's amateurish care for the better part of a week. He had tolerated Karen's brief presence in the house twice a day only because she opened cans he could not open on his own. Otherwise, he had no use for her and rarely bothered to make an appearance when she arrived.

As soon as Grant walked into the house, Rajah began expressing his displeasure over the long absence. He began by jumping onto the kitchen island and retching up a hairball the size of a python. While Grant tended to that mess, one hand over his mouth and the other wrapped in a dish towel, Rajah strolled into the living room and began shredding the corner of the luxurious couch. He had never done so before and immediately realized he shouldn't have waited so long. Silk shredded so easily.

Rajah kept scratching until Grant ran into the living room and yelled for him to stop. Then he bolted across the room, leapt onto the sheer curtains, and began climbing. When he reached the top, he hung there by his front claws until the fabric gave way under his weight. The hole was nearly a foot long by the time Grant raced over and chased him toward the foyer, where Rajah promptly jumped into the largest planter and, with a look of immense satisfaction, used it as a litter box.

Having stated his case in terms Grant could understand, Rajah calmly went to the kitchen and flopped on the floor next to his brush, waiting to be groomed properly for the first time in several days. He purred loudly when the brushing began, a signal that the brief revolt was over, at least until the next time he was left to Karen's care.

An hour and a half passed before Grant was able to sit down at the laptop and craft the outline that was in his head. But when he did, the words flowed easily. Two college professors, both in search of happiness, had the good fortune to meet and fall in love. The path they traveled was filled with obstacles, as such paths always are, but they beat the odds and proved that sometimes love can, in fact, conquer all.

It was comfortably trite and sappy, precisely the sort of thing a large segment of romance readers would fall in love with. He was confident that if he succeeded in transforming his lead characters into appealing, believable, three-dimensional beings, the book would be a huge success.

Now all he needed was fifty or sixty chapters of sparkling prose.

To a man in love, everything seemed possible.

37.

Grackle sat alone in the back of the black SUV, badly shaken after being arrested at Newark Liberty for cybertheft and informed that she faced up to twenty years in federal prison. In the front seat were Jorge Suarez and Marla Kincaid, who tag-teamed their highly confused prisoner with nonstop questions during the one-hour drive to Steinville. She was either a victim or a felon, and they were determined to find out which.

"Where did you first meet Oleg Gruzdev?"

She claimed she had never heard the name.

"When did you meet James Corcoran?"

They had bumped into each other in Steinville one day, she told them, when he was in town finalizing the purchase of a local company. He asked her to dinner, and they fell in love.

"When did you and he decide to steal two million dollars from the college?"

Crying now, she said she had never stolen anything from anyone.

"When did you open your Swiss bank account?"

She swore she did not even know how to open a Swiss bank account.

"Where is he now?"

She provided the details of her ill-fated visit to Bermuda and Corcoran's promise to meet her there. She didn't know where he was, but she fervently hoped he would spend the rest of his life in prison followed by eternity in hell's fires.

After grilling her throughout the entire trip, the agents satisfied themselves that Grackle had been manipulated by a clever Russian criminal—or, as Suarez had thoughtlessly put it, *played like an old fiddle.* Then they explained exactly how Gruzdev, aka Corcoran, had managed to get his hands on Hickston's two million dollars. Once he had gained

149

access to the college's computer system, he decided it would be best if he could get her out of the country while his scheme worked its magic, so he lured her to Bermuda with the promise of everlasting love. That way she would be temporarily unavailable to the FBI and the local police when the money was reported stolen. Even better, her absence might make her look like the person who had stolen it. Having guided the operation masterfully from start to finish, he was now in the wind, most likely searching for his next victim.

"I thought he loved me," Grackle said sorrowfully as the SUV pulled to the curb in front of her house.

"That's typically how guys like him operate," Suarez said. "It's the oldest trick in the book."

"What happens to me now?"

"You won't hear from the FBI again unless we find Gruzdev and need your testimony."

"Am I in trouble with the college?"

"Not my call. I'll let President Farnsworth know you're back in town, and the rest is between you and him."

Twenty minutes after opening her front door and pouring herself a tumbler of vodka, she took a phone call from Sarah Townsend. Farnsworth's secretary told her to appear at 9:00 sharp the next morning for a confidential discussion. After a sleepless night filled with tears and profound regret, she took her raging hangover to the president's office and found three stone-faced men waiting there for her. Joining Farnsworth for the session were Dean Byron Shuttleworth and Hickston's security director, Rex Dunbar.

Dunbar kicked things off by quoting the relevant passage from the user agreement she had signed at the time she was given access to the school's computer system: *I agree I will not use, share, or store applications other than those provided by the college's IT department.*

"Does that ring a bell?" Dunbar snapped.

"I remember signing something," she answered miserably, "but I don't remember the specific language. I definitely didn't use any unauthorized applications."

He handed her a printout of the email Corcoran had sent her.

"You were using Hickston's system at the time you downloaded the software that Corcoran or Gruzdev or whatever his name is sent you.

That software ultimately invited him into our system and allowed him to steal two million dollars."

"I didn't know."

"Now you do," Shuttleworth chimed in, "and in light of your egregious violation of college policy, I'm terminating your contract effective immediately."

"But I have tenure!" she protested.

"You *had* tenure. You're being terminated for gross misconduct leading to the loss of two million dollars."

Between tears she managed to say, "I'm sorry."

"Your apology won't replace the two million dollars that were stolen from us," Farnsworth grumbled. "There's a straight line between your unauthorized action and Hickston's financial loss, and you alone are responsible for what happened. Our attorney will decide whether to pursue this in court."

The meeting ended with Dunbar confiscating her faculty ID card and office keys. When she complained that she had personal belongings in the office—books, research notes, and other evidence of her years at Hickston—he told her that such items would be shipped to her only after a rigorous internal investigation into whether she had committed any other crimes against the college.

As Grackle was leaving the campus in disgrace, Shuttleworth was placing a call to Professor Georgette Mealey, who was in her backyard tending to a small vegetable garden that seemed to be coming along nicely. He told her about Grackle's downfall, then asked her to serve, as she had done ten years earlier, as the English department's chairperson. She accepted graciously, then immediately phoned Professor Thurston Grunwald, her old friend and the man who had recently chaired the tenure committee.

She had an idea that might interest him.

38.

The members of Hickston's tenure committee gathered two days after Grackle had been fired, and taking her place at the session was Georgette Mealey, the new English department head. Chairman Thurston Grunwald called the meeting to order for the purpose of re-considering Grant's previously declined application, and Mealey spoke on his behalf, saying all the things Grackle should have said but had not.

He was a promising writer who also happened to have the highest student ratings of any Hickston faculty member. In addition, he was a kind and likable person who helped create a supportive and collegial campus atmosphere. He had, in short, demonstrated all the qualities the college wanted its faculty members to possess. Despite this, or perhaps even because of it, he had been abused and lied to by the English department's former chairperson. The tenure committee now had an opportunity to right a terrible wrong.

The vote came after minimal discussion, and the committee members quickly returned to their summer vacations. All but Georgette Mealey, that is. Before leaving the campus, she phoned Grant, who at that moment was working his way through an important chapter of his first romance. He let the call go to voicemail so as not to break his concentration. Whoever it was could undoubtedly wait until he wrote another few hundred words.

His two protagonists, both college professors, were confronting a serious problem. What appeared to be a simple case of love at first sight was complicated by an inconvenient fact: the woman was already engaged to a man she liked a great deal but did not truly love. The chapter in question was therefore devoted to her growing sense of guilt over her feelings for the second man. Should she break things off with her fiancé, a good man who had done nothing to deserve being mistreated, or should she marry him even though her heart now belonged to someone else? Grant handled the woman's inner conflict with great sensitivity, successfully portraying a complex, three-dimensional character who hated herself for being disloyal to the man she had promised to marry.

Forty minutes later, with the chapter completed in rough form, Grant listened to the voice message.

"Hello, Grant. This is Georgette. Hannah Grackle is no longer employed by Hickston College, and I was named to replace her. I met a few minutes ago with the tenure committee, and we reviewed your application a second time. I am pleased to report that you were granted tenure by a unanimous vote. Please call me when you have a moment so that we can have you reinstated as a member of the Hickston faculty. Congratulations, Grant! I look forward to working with you again."

It was a stunning and wholly unexpected turn of events. A minute earlier he had been writing about a fictional character's inner turmoil, and now he was experiencing the same thing firsthand. He had already put his old life behind him and was on his way to creating something new and, he hoped, better. At the same time, though, he remembered the exhilaration he had felt a few weeks earlier after being told, mistakenly, that he had been granted tenure. He had been over-the-moon happy then, and part of him was again. Like the woman in his novel, he couldn't decide whether he should be faithful to the old, safe love or risk everything for the new, exciting one.

Instead of phoning Georgette, he called Miranda, who had become his faithful guide on the new journey. He stood before two roads, he told her, like the person in Robert Frost's "The Road Not Taken." Should he choose the safe one or the one less traveled?

"This is not an either/or decision," she said without hesitation. "Unlike the speaker in the poem, you can travel both roads, which was your plan all along. You were going to be a professor who also wrote novels, and now that door has been reopened for you. You're an excellent teacher and belong in the classroom. But you're also an excellent writer who needs to fulfill that part of his destiny. If you say no to tenure, it's a permanent no. Why close that door unnecessarily?"

"I was hoping you would say something like that," he admitted, "but I was afraid you might feel as though you had just wasted a whole lot of time on my romance education."

"The education wasn't wasted as long as you keep writing."

"You're absolutely right." He paused for a moment. "And, look, we're still in June, so I have plenty of time to finish the novel. At the current pace, I should be ready to publish it before the fall semester begins."

"Then call Georgette and tell her you're coming back!"

"I will."

"Excellent. Then the celebration dinner is on me tonight. Come to my house at 6:00, okay?"

"Want me to bring anything?"

"Your appetite."

"Which one?" he asked suggestively.

"All of them."

Grant's conversation with his new department chairperson lasted nearly an hour and was a refreshing change from his infrequent and always unpleasant sessions with Grackle. Georgette planned to add additional creative writing courses suited to his talents, and she would make sure he received a six-month sabbatical within the next year. In addition to the larger paycheck that came with becoming an associate professor, he would get a better office. Grackle's old office, in fact. Georgette said she liked the office she already had and wasn't interested in moving.

"So how's the writing?" she asked. "Alicia Fillip has been spreading a rumor that you're now a proud pornographer."

"I'm not," he assured her. He didn't bother mentioning the salacious story that Miranda had trashed.

"I didn't think so."

"I'm writing a love story, actually. It's hardly what I would call serious literature, but I don't see anything wrong with popular fiction that's written well."

"I couldn't agree more. I've read every Nora Roberts novel, some of them three times."

"Do you ever watch Hallmark movies?"

"Grant, all women watch Hallmark movies even if they don't admit it. Shakespeare they're not," she noted, "but, then, I'm not always in the mood for Shakespeare. On a different subject entirely, how's Miranda these days?"

"Absolutely wonderful."

"She is wonderful, isn't she? And I take it she's your muse."

"I hadn't really thought of her that way, but, yes, I suppose she is."

"Two Hickston professors fall in love and live happily ever after. I'd gladly read that story."

"If I write it," he promised, "you'll be one of the first to see it."

"I'll hold you to that, Grant. See you on campus before long."

Only after the call ended did he marvel at the fact that Georgette had referred to Miranda as his muse.

Apparently, good news traveled fast on the Hickston campus.

39.

It wasn't only good news that traveled fast on the Hickston campus. A few days after his unpleasant meeting with the board of trustees, Farnsworth heard through the campus grapevine that the investigation into his leadership wasn't going at all well.

According to the rumor, a highly credible one, his management practices were getting extraordinarily low marks, and his unintended role in the recent loss of two million dollars was only one example. Hickston's buildings, for instance, were found to be grossly underinsured because he had refused to pay for more coverage. Water was dripping from too many ceilings in too many classrooms because building maintenance wasn't one of his priorities. And the college's endowment had failed to benefit from one of the most remarkable periods in the U.S. stock market's history because he foolishly considered corporate bonds a better investment. These and other managerial failures pointed to the unavoidable conclusion that the board was on the verge of firing him.

But he had a strategy that might save his skin.

He went to Arthur Sproull's office and walked in unannounced just as his vice president for development was lining up a long, tricky putt. Sproull dropped the putter and nearly wet himself when the president cleared his throat.

"I d-d-do this only at lunchtime," Sproull stuttered, as he always did when frightened.

"B-b-but it's only 10:00 a.m.," Farnsworth mocked. "D-d-do you get my drift?"

Sproull nodded. "How can I help you?" he asked submissively.

"By telling me where we stand with that forty-million-dollar bequest we're supposed to get from Beatrice Hagfeldt. You told me she would be dead within two weeks, and I still haven't seen her obituary in the local rag."

"Yes, I've been meaning to update you on the situation."

"Only if it's convenient," Farnsworth said caustically. "I apologize for interrupting your golf game."

"I swear I don't usually practice in the office."

"Beatrice Hagfeldt!" Farnsworth screamed.

"Yes, of course. I'm pleased to report that she's on her deathbed. I went to see her yesterday just as the doctor was walking out. Her vital signs are failing, and she seems to be in a great deal of pain. So this is all quite positive. A few more days and she's history."

Farnsworth smiled for the first time. "Excellent. Then here's how you and I are going to handle this, Arthur. The board of trustees is attempting to play hardball with me," he explained, "and Beatrice is my ace in the hole. I intend to let the board chairman know that if I get dumped, the forty-million-dollar bequest goes away. Are we clear?"

Sproull looked confused. "But you've never even met Beatrice."

"I didn't have to. She's leaving us the money because she values all the things I have done for Hickston and for Steinville. If it weren't for me, the money would be going elsewhere. Isn't that true?"

Farnsworth's murderous eyes guided Sproull to the correct response.

"Yes, of course. You're the reason she made Hickston her sole beneficiary."

"And you will quietly adjust the terms of the will to state that her bequest is contingent upon my continued employment as Hickston's president, won't you?"

"Immediately."

"And then we'll never mention this brief conversation to anyone, will we?"

"Absolutely not. It's our secret."

"Good. I knew I could count you on, Arthur. After all, a wrong word from me, and you would never work in higher education again, would you?"

"I understand, Porter. My lips are sealed."

Sproull waited for Farnsworth to leave the building, then checked the ten-thousand-dollar recording system he had installed years earlier to document his conversations with donors. The sound was crystal clear: *"Here's how you and I are going to handle this, Arthur."*

Not until two days later did Farnsworth finally receive the call he had been expecting from Herman Withers, chairman of Hickston's board. He allowed Withers to ramble on for several minutes about the investigation, the troubling evidence of flimsy risk-management policies, and a number of personal expenses that board members considered suspect. Among the most alarming expenses, Withers pointed out, was a fifteen-thousand-dollar set of graphite golf clubs, each one monogrammed, of course.

When he had finally heard enough, Farnsworth interrupted Withers with, "It's time to switch subjects, Herman. Let's talk about a certain forty-million-dollar gift that Hickston will receive shortly, but only if I'm here to accept it."

In Farnsworth's version of the story, he was the sole reason his old friend Beatrice Hagfeldt had named the college as her beneficiary. He had nurtured the relationship carefully while president, he explained, and Hickston now stood at the threshold of a new era of accomplishment fueled by stock worth forty million dollars, possibly even more.

"My primary role here is to raise money," he told Withers. "The president of a college is always the most important fundraiser, as you well know, and I have done that job brilliantly. Of course, if the board decides for any reason to interfere with my good work, Beatrice Hagfeldt's generous gift will be the first victim of such foolishness. She has made it clear that the gift is contingent upon my being president."

The normally loquacious Withers was at a loss for words. Weeks earlier he had heard that a forty-million-dollar gift might be forthcoming, but this was the first time he had been told it was the direct result of Farnsworth's efforts. The fact that the gift was contingent upon Farnsworth's continued employment created a dilemma since the full board had already voted unanimously for his termination. Allowing Farnsworth to retain the presidency presented clear risks but so did walking away from a forty-million-dollar gift.

Withers decided that receiving the money was more important than getting rid of Farnsworth.

"You misunderstand my purpose in calling, Porter. The board has given no thought whatsoever to changing Hickston's leadership. We merely want to point out certain issues that I'm sure can be remedied in short order."

"In that case, I look forward to receiving the committee's list of recommendations, and I will faithfully address each of them as swiftly as possible."

"Then we're in full agreement," Withers said, struggling to sound cheerful. "Good luck with the huge bequest. It certainly comes at a good time, doesn't it?"

"The timing could not possibly be better, Herman."

40.

Except for those hours when Grant was writing—three hours in the morning and three more in the afternoon—he and Miranda were inseparable. They ate breakfast together every day, usually at his place after having spent the night together in the vibrating bed that Naomi had thoughtfully mentioned to Miranda. Then they cared for Naomi's plants, dividing the chore so that Grant would have more time to work on his novel. While Grant wrote, Miranda either ran errands or read books that she might decide to use when the new academic year began. And at the end of each day they either cooked together or went out for dinner.

In other words, they spent enough time together to gain some meaningful insights into each other's many quirks.

Miranda learned, for instance, that Grant seemed genetically opposed to change. He grew distressed when Kellogg's redesigned his favorite cereal box, and he became downright distraught when he learned that Mike Krzyzewski was retiring after forty-seven glorious years of coaching basketball. For him, Coach K's retirement was like having the sun rise in the west and set in the east. It was unnatural.

Grant, meanwhile, learned that Miranda enjoyed shopping all day every day even if she didn't need anything, which helped explain why she had a house filled with things she would never use even if she lived to one hundred, which seemed probable given her rigorous exercise routine. The only saving grace was that most of the useless things she bought— obscure kitchen devices, trendy fitness shoes that never got worn, an ultrasonic toothbrush that even a physicist would find too complicated to use—were inexpensive. But still. For a man who hated shopping, the behavior was inexplicable.

Nevertheless, after weeks of being with each other almost constantly, they agreed they were a perfect match. Their differences were small, their similarities large and wonderful. Although they tried not to overthink the relationship, they had fallen into a comfortable union that under the right circumstances could easily lead to marriage. They both knew it even while avoiding the M word.

The catalyst for a major change in their relationship was a call from Israel. Naomi phoned Miranda to say her archeological efforts had resulted in an unexpected find: an Israeli man with whom she had fallen hopelessly in love. Like her, the man was an archaeology professor. Also like her, he was wealthy, an only child who had inherited a fortune from his industrialist father. They agreed to keep their assets separate and live happily ever after, mostly in the desert searching for buried history.

Much of the one-hour call was devoted to Naomi's plan to sell her home in Steinville. She and husband-to-be Aaron Weiss would be dividing their time between a relatively modest home in Tel Aviv and his opulent waterfront villa in Santorini, which was an ideal jumping-off point for archeological digs in Athens. As soon as she heard that Grant had been rehired by Hickston, she said she would gladly sell him the home for what she had paid for it years earlier since she didn't need to turn a profit on the transaction. Her only goal was to get rid of the place fast so that she could move on with her new life.

She told Miranda that she and Aaron would fly to New York soon, pack up the few things she wanted to keep, and then return to Israel with Rajah. If Grant wanted the fully furnished home at a bargain price, she would gladly hold the mortgage. If he wasn't interested, she would put the place on the market as soon as Grant had found another place to live.

When Grant finished writing for the day, Miranda told him about her conversation with Naomi, thereby triggering a prolonged discussion of where their relationship was headed. If they intended to be a permanent couple, they obviously didn't need two Steinville homes. Otherwise, they did. In that case, buying Naomi's home would be the best financial deal of Grant's life.

They tabled the discussion until after dinner, when over a glass of wine Grant told Miranda what was on his mind.

"When I was unemployed and wondering whether I could support myself as a writer," he began, "I felt I was in no position to make serious plans for the future. But now that I have tenure and a better salary, I am. And what I want the future to hold is us. I want you to marry me, Miranda."

She put her glass down and took both his hands in hers.

"Is that a formal proposal?" she asked softly.

"It is."

"Then I formally accept."

"You do?"

"I do."

"Then tomorrow we need to buy a ring."

She smiled. "It's early. The stores are still open."

"Right, I meant tonight we need to buy a ring."

"And you'll actually go shopping with me?"

"For this, yes."

"Good. I know just the place."

Miranda knew the place because twice recently she had walked past Steinville Jewelers and peered in the window at the latest offerings in engagement rings. Her ex had purchased her first engagement ring without her input, which is why she had ended up with a gaudy five-carat round diamond that was too big for her hand. This time she wanted something more tasteful and better suited to a college professor than to a Saudi princess.

Grant surprised her when he scanned the display case and pointed to an elegant emerald-cut ring, the same one that had caught her eye a week earlier.

"You like that one?" she asked.

"I do, but it's your call."

She slipped the two-carat ring on her finger, checked her hand in the mirror, and smiled. The ring looked fabulous, and, better still, it happened to fit perfectly. A quick swipe of Grant's credit card made it hers.

They agreed she should wear it home. They also agreed to stop on the way to buy a split of champagne.

Tonight they would celebrate in style.

41.

At 6:15 a.m. on June 21st, an ambulance raced Beatrice Hagfeldt to Steinville Hospital, where she died an hour later after her long, grueling battle with cancer. As the old woman was taking her last raspy breath, Sproull was wringing his hands and praying fervently in the hospital waiting room, having been notified by Wanda, Beatrice's live-in care-giver, that it looked as though this was the end. Since Beatrice had no living family members, she had left instructions for Sproull to be called when her time to go was imminent.

The young doctor in the white lab coat stifled a yawn as he entered the waiting room. He had been up all night presiding over the deaths of three old people, each of whom had been granted months or years of extra suffering through the miracle of modern medicine. He forced a sad smile before speaking.

"Are you here for Beatrice Hagfeldt?" he asked solemnly.

"Yes, I'm Arthur Sproull from Hickston College."

"I'm afraid she didn't make it. The pancreatic cancer had spread to the liver, and no treatment was possible. I'm sorry."

Sproull hung his head. "I'm sorry as well. She was a wonderful woman. Thank you for doing what you could."

Sproull waited for the doctor to leave the room before pumping his fist and saying, "Thank you, God!" under his breath. He waited until he had reached the parking lot before calling Farnsworth, who was still lying in bed alongside Alicia Fillip when his cell phone rang.

"Have you lost your mind, Arthur?" Farnsworth snapped, grabbing the call on the first ring. Alicia was still snoring. "Do you know what time it is?"

"Time to celebrate, Porter. Our friend Beatrice has finally kicked the bucket."

"Oh, my. Well, that certainly is worth celebrating, isn't it?" Farnsworth crept from the bedroom and walked to the kitchen to turn on the Keurig machine. "She took her sweet old time about it, didn't she?"

"Water over the dam, Porter. She's gone now, and the Curetell Sciences stock will soon be ours."

"How long before we get it?"

"A day or two. The will is quite simple. All the stock and the money in her bank account come to the college. End of story."

"You didn't mention her house. What about that?"

"Unfortunately, she decided a week ago to leave the house to her money-grubbing caregiver. But the house is a wreck anyway. More trouble than it's worth."

"Can't we contest the changed will and get the house?"

"We could try," Sproull noted, "but that would hold up the stock transfer."

"No, let's not go there. It just feels like robbery to me. She promised us that house."

"We have forty million dollars coming in, Porter."

"And the first million of it is going to be spent updating this dump I live in. Alicia and I have big plans for the place. New kitchen, new master bath, a lap pool, and more furniture."

"I see no reason why we can't set aside two million," Sproull chuckled. "It's the most important building on campus, after all."

"And you're sure you took care of that little detail we discussed?" Farnsworth asked conspiratorially.

"Absolutely. The will specifies that the stock comes to Hickston only if you're the president."

"Good man. Your annual salary is going to rise sharply, my friend."

As soon as Farnsworth returned to the bedroom, Alicia asked why he was wandering through the house at such an ungodly hour. He told her.

"I also specified that the first two million will be spent on upgrading our home."

"Lovely idea, Porter. I could also use a new car."

"A Porsche 911 convertible, perhaps?"

She grinned. "That might work. Why don't we discuss this further in bed?"

Farnsworth and Alicia were still in bed celebrating Hickston's windfall when at 9:10 a.m. the U.S. Justice Department announced that the CEO of Curetell Sciences had been charged with ten counts of wire fraud. The evidence was clear: the company had released and then actively promoted false test results for its totally ineffective cancer vaccine. Far from preventing cancer, the vaccine had been shown by government scientists to *cause* cancer in a large percentage of lab animals.

By the time the New York Stock Exchange opened at 9:30, Curetell was selling for one cent per share, down from three hundred dollars per share the previous day, making Beatrice Hagfeldt's bequest worth slightly more than one thousand dollars instead of forty million. A few minutes after the opening bell, the stock was officially worthless.

Among the few people to have earned a fortune on Curetell's stock before the collapse was the company's CEO, who was already living under an assumed name at his fifteen-million-dollar villa in Punta Del Este.

A man could live quite well on two billion dollars in Uruguay.

Also at 9:30 that morning all eleven members of Hickston's board of trustees, unaware of the collapse of Curetell Sciences stock, were meeting secretly off campus to address an alarming issue that had just been raised by Edward Toomey, attorney for the late Beatrice Hagfeldt. He claimed to have seen an altered copy of his client's will in which someone had made handwritten changes to certain key terms. Among the changes, he said, was that her bequest to Hickston was contingent upon Porter Farnsworth's continued employment as president.

Toomey had delivered the message by phone to board chairman Herman Withers a few minutes after Beatrice's death, and Withers found the story almost impossible to believe.

"Are handwritten changes to a will legal?" Withers had asked.

"Under certain circumstances, yes," Toomey had replied. "In this instance, no."

"Why not?"

"Because at the time Beatrice allegedly made the changes and dated the document, she was in a coma. And she remained in that coma until she died this morning at Steinville Hospital."

Without naming his source, Toomey had then helpfully pointed out that one of the last people to visit Beatrice in her final days was Hickston's vice president for institutional advancement, Arthur Sproull.

165

Following a brief and turbulent meeting, the board members drove to the Hickston campus and paraded to Farnsworth's office. When they walked in without knocking, they found him seated at a round conference table with an architect who was suggesting ways in which the president's house could be improved by an investment of two million dollars.

Sensing an impending storm, the architect gathered his sketches and hastily departed, leaving Farnsworth to the board's mercy. But mercy was in short supply. Chairman Withers demanded to know who had changed Beatrice Hagfeldt's will and who had authorized the fraud.

"I know absolutely nothing about this," Farnsworth insisted. "Beatrice, may she rest in peace, told me only that she was leaving her fortune in Curetell Sciences stock to Hickston. We never discussed the details of her will."

Before Withers could challenge Farnsworth's statement, Arthur Sproull appeared at the doorway looking ashen. Seeing the terror written on the president's face did nothing to buoy his spirits.

"I-I'll c-c-come back," he muttered before Withers ordered him into the room.

"We were just talking with Porter about Beatrice Hagfeldt's bequest," Withers observed icily. "Since you're here now, why not tell us what you know?"

"I c-c-came here as soon as I heard the news."

"That Beatrice had died?"

He shook his head. "That the Curetell Sciences stock is now w-w-worthless." The look of disbelief on a dozen faces suggested to Sproull that he had misunderstood the question. "That's what you're talking about, isn't it?"

"No," Withers told him, "we were talking about the fraudulent handwritten changes to Beatrice's will."

"I didn't want to do it," Sproull wailed, "but Porter threatened me."

"He's lying, of course," Farnsworth said casually. "I have never done anything illegal in my entire life."

Sproull removed the cell phone from the inside pocket of his suit jacket, clicked on the voice recorder app, and hit PLAY.

"And you will quietly adjust the terms of the bequest to state that it is contingent upon my continued employment as Hickston's president, won't you?"

"Immediately."

"And then we'll never mention this brief conversation of ours to anyone, will we?"

"Absolutely not. It's our secret."

"Good. I knew I could count you on, Arthur. After all, a wrong word from me, and you would never work in higher education again, would you?"

Farnsworth's face turned beet red and his eyes bulged as he lunged for Sproull. The two youngest members of the board, both former Hickston football players, restrained him while Withers called 911.

Farnsworth and Sproull were officially unemployed by the time they had been arrested by the Steinville police and led from the president's office in handcuffs.

Now all the board had to do was find a qualified leader dumb enough to take on the challenge of a scandal-ridden, nearly broke college whose only asset of note was a championship basketball team.

42.

They awoke later than usual having spent the previous night celebrating their engagement. Rajah was miraculously compliant, skipping his customary 6:30 a.m. demand for nourishment as though he knew this was an important day. And, indeed, it was.

Grant and Miranda had reached a decision before falling asleep. They would buy Naomi's home and sell Miranda's, using the cash from the sale for a vacation home, most likely at Lake George. Their two Hickston salaries would allow them to pay off a mortgage on Naomi's home within ten years, possibly sooner. Anything Grant earned from his first novel would be icing on the cake.

While Grant was inside toiling over chapter twenty-three, Miranda was on a long, joyous call with Naomi. A few months ago, and for different reasons, the two friends had all but given up on the idea of falling in love. Now they were both getting married. Naomi would marry first because she and Aaron had decided on an August wedding, a lavish event with hundreds of family and friends in attendance. Grant and Naomi were leaning toward December and a small reception for family and close friends.

A few minutes before noon, Grant was roaming the kitchen in search of something to eat when Miranda came in from the patio and told him that the deal with Naomi had been struck. All that remained was helping Naomi and Aaron pack a few things when they flew in the following week. Since there was nothing especially appetizing in the refrigerator, they decided to celebrate their home purchase with lunch at Margot's Grill. They didn't love Margot's, but the food was adequate and the service fast.

On this particular day, however, the food was not the primary topic of conversation at the restaurant. The small dining room was abuzz with word that Farnsworth and Sproull had been fired. It was still a rumor, but the source was none other than Rex Dunbar, the college's security director, who had left Margot's a few minutes earlier after finishing a large portion of the day's special, shepherd's pie.

After placing their lunch order—a cheeseburger for Grant, a grilled Reuben for Miranda—Grant called Jim McArdle, who always seemed to have the inside scoop when it came to campus news. Was there any truth to the rumor that Farnsworth and Sproull were history?

"You should drop whatever novel you're working on," McArdle laughed, "and write this story instead."

He then provided the sordid details. At Farnsworth's direction, Sproull had falsified Beatrice Hagfeldt's will, thereby making both of them criminals. Then Beatrice's stock in Curetell Sciences, once worth forty million dollars, had become utterly worthless. Although Jim didn't share the name of the staff member who had given him the full story, Grant assumed it was Sarah Townsend, Farnsworth's secretary and Dana McArdle's first cousin.

"So this was the gigantic gift that Farnsworth bragged about at the faculty meeting," Grant said.

"The very same."

"So what happens now?"

"The board tries to find a new president, and the fundraisers try to find the next Beatrice Hagfeldt. And let's hope there's success on both fronts," Jim added, "because I'm not hearing good things about Hickston's financial situation."

"Really?"

"Yes, really. If things don't turn around quickly, we could all be pounding the pavement."

Not one to let bad news ruin a meal, Grant polished off his cheeseburger while he and Miranda debated what the news could mean for them personally. They refrained from hitting the panic button, but they agreed that this would be a good time for Grant to get his first novel ready for publication since book sales might be the only income they could count on in the near future.

"Then I guess it's time for you to read the latest draft," he said.

"Agreed. As soon as we get home."

Alone on the sunny patio, Miranda breezed through the first twenty-two chapters of *The Professors of Love* and decided it was one of the most engaging romances she had read in years. The characters were believable and likable, and the writing was crisp, fluid, and contemporary. As far as she was concerned, there was only one significant problem that needed to be addressed.

"What's that?" Grant asked when she came back inside to offer her critique.

"Tell me if you've heard this story. A woman is already engaged but falls in love with someone else. She wonders whether she should break things off with her fiancé, a kind man who doesn't deserve to be mistreated, or should marry him even though her heart now belongs to someone else. In the movie version, she ends up running through Manhattan to the Empire State Building."

"Oh, my God," he groaned. "I've been writing a knockoff of *Sleepless in Seattle.*"

"To a certain extent, yes. But this is completely fixable," she insisted. "All you have to do is change a few facts. For example, let's assume the woman isn't engaged. Maybe she was dumped by her previous boyfriend and is wondering whether she'll ever be able to trust another man."

"But that would basically be the same story."

"It's *always* basically the same story, Grant. Boy and girl meet, boy and girl fall in love, boy and girl live happily ever after unless we're talking about *Romeo and Juliet* or *West Side Story.* The core plot never really changes," she said, "and romance readers never get tired of it. Make a few changes, and your story will no longer be *Sleepless in Seattle.*"

"You think it's that simple?"

"I wouldn't say so otherwise. This book is going to be a huge hit."

"I hope you're right, especially if Hickston's finances are as bad as Jim believes. Tenure won't mean anything if Hickston fails."

Her smile slowly turned into a frown. "I can tell you as a member of the town council that Steinville can't afford to have the college close its doors. If Hickston fails," she said flatly, "Steinville fails. It's as simple as that. But if things are as bad as Jim says, I can't see the board finding a first-rate candidate for the presidency."

"Unless," he countered, "they look in-house and select someone who has chaired an academic department while helping revitalize

Steinville as a member of the town council. As I've said before, you would be perfect for the job."

"It's not one I want."

"You wouldn't take the job even if doing so meant saving both the college and the town?"

"You're blinded by love, Grant. I'm not the person who can save them."

"I respectfully disagree. Hickston needs a proven leader who has impeccable academic credentials and is capable of functioning in the real world. That's you."

She thought for a moment before saying, "Tell you what. You go back to writing, and I'll give the idea some thought."

"You're not just saying that to get rid of me, right?"

She grinned. "Not entirely."

It wasn't the answer he had hoped for, but he could tell it was the best he was going to get at the moment. While he set about revising *Professors in Love*, she returned to the patio armed with a felt-tip pen and a yellow legal pad.

She had some ideas she thought might be worth jotting down.

43.

The Hickston College board of trustees announced an application deadline of July 1st for those interested in being the school's next president. Not surprisingly, the first resumes to arrive came almost exclusively from a group of bona fide losers who had helped run other colleges into the ground. All of them blamed their previous failures on factors beyond their control—weak trustees, poor locations, competing institutions— and claimed to deserve a chance to test their mettle one more time.

The only truly qualified outside candidate was a man who currently served as president of a prosperous small college in Ohio. He said he was willing to consider the Hickston position for an annual salary of two million dollars and a five-year, no-cut contract. Since the man in question was sixty-seven years old, the board correctly assumed that all he really wanted was a fat compensation package that would allow him to retire in style. He was not invited to interview for the position.

At 4:30 p.m. on June 30th, Miranda delivered her application package in person to Herman Withers, who was hanging out in the president's office on a part-time basis while he and his board colleagues screened resumes. She and Withers had sat next to each other at a campus reception two years earlier, and he remembered her as the French professor who had been remarkably well-versed in the political, economic, and cultural affairs of Steinville. She was a member of the town council, he vaguely recalled, and had sound ideas for improving the local community's fortunes.

She thanked him for considering her credentials and gave him a firm handshake before leaving. The meeting was brief but, at least for Withers, highly impactful. Everything about her—the probing eyes, the commanding voice, the smart blue business suit—fit his image of a college president. She was young, of course, but so were some of the country's most successful entrepreneurs. At the very least, she wasn't someone who viewed the Hickston presidency as a comfortable retirement home of sorts. Miranda struck Withers as a woman on a mission who brought far more to the table than the retreads who had submitted their resumes so far.

The package she had left with him confirmed his instincts. In addition to the customary cover letter and glowing resume, she had included a ten-page analysis of Hickston's primary strengths and weaknesses. The document detailed the steps she would take to capitalize on what the college did best while eliminating the things it did worst. Importantly, her recommendations focused on the critical role that Hickston and Steinville each played in the other's future. If one failed, she said, the other would fail. But together they could become one of those rare instances in which one plus one equals three.

"Well, I did it," Miranda told Grant when she returned home. "But I'm still not sure why."

"You did it for two reasons," he said, wrapping his arms around her. "First, you're not willing to let Hickston close its doors forever. Second, we both know you can do the job better than anyone else. So now what?"

"Now I wait. I spoke briefly with Herman Withers, and he said the board wanted to have the new president in place well before September."

"I predict you'll hear soon."

She shrugged and said, "I don't think so, but we'll see. In the meantime, I need to buy a few things for our new home. Want to come?"

"I haven't been good enough," he joked. "I think I'll write while you shop."

Their new home was the one they had bought a few days earlier when Naomi and Aaron had flown in from Israel by private jet. As far as anyone could tell, Aaron was the only archeologist on the planet worth seven billion dollars. He was completely unimpressed by the wealth since he had merely inherited it, but he was willing to spend lavishly on Naomi's behalf. So he had decided that traveling by private jet made the most sense since they would be returning to Israel with several large crates of her belongings as well as a cat named Rajah. A private jet also made it possible for them to cart off Naomi's beloved collection of house plants, all of which had been thriving under Grant's care.

The day after Naomi and Aaron had flown back to Israel, Miranda put her house on the market and received ten offers within twenty-four hours. Because all the offers were above asking price, it looked as though she and Grant would be able to pay cash for a vacation home when they decided to buy. They planned to hold off on that idea, though, until Hickston's future became clearer.

"Whatever I buy today," she said playfully before leaving, "you'll have to live with for a long time. Are you sure you don't want to help pick things out?"

"Things like curtains, rugs, and dishes?"

"Exactly."

"I have no opinion on things like that. But I do have an opinion on another important subject."

"Which is?"

"Why are we waiting until December to get married? We own a home, we're in love, and there's no reason to wait."

His suggestion was totally unexpected, and Miranda's face showed it. "When were you thinking?"

"Why not today? We drive into town, get a license, and have the mayor preside."

"I think there's a mandatory waiting period after you get the license."

"Twenty-four hours, but a town judge can waive that. I'm sure you're friends with a few judges because of your work on the town council."

"We had talked about having a small reception."

"We can have people here for a combination wedding reception and housewarming."

She pondered the idea for a few moments, then smiled. "That would work."

They sealed the deal with a kiss before driving into town in the Mercedes that Naomi had thrown in with the house at no extra charge. At 3:30 p.m., by the power vested in Steinville Mayor Charles Dinwoody, Grant and Miranda became husband and wife.

They didn't know it yet, but things were about to get seriously interesting.

44.

Grant phoned Les Bois on the way home from the brief marriage ceremony only to be told that the restaurant was fully booked for the evening. But when he mentioned the special occasion, the reservationist transferred his call to the owner.

"If you come at 6:30," the owner said immediately, "we'll have a lovely table for you and your bride."

They went home and changed into something suitable for a fancy French restaurant, then drove off for their wedding-night dinner. At 6:20 p.m. they were pulling into the restaurant's parking lot when Miranda's phone rang. She didn't recognize the number, but she took the call as soon as she saw the name.

"This is Herman Withers, Miranda," the board chairman said when she answered. "I hope I'm not calling at a bad time."

"Not at all, Chairman Withers. How can I help you?"

She looked over at Grant, who gave her a thumbs-up.

"I'm wondering whether you would be available to meet with the presidential search committee tomorrow morning at 10:00."

"Tomorrow at 10:00 would be fine. Where's the meeting?"

"In the boardroom down the hall from the president's office."

"I know the place," she said pleasantly. "I'll be there at 10:00. Thank you for the invitation."

"My pleasure. Have a good evening."

"Thank you. You as well."

Grant waited until she hung up, then said, "Did I predict you would hear from them soon?"

"I'm sure they're just being overly courteous because I'm a faculty member."

"They're not just being courteous, Miranda. The package you submitted was obviously head and shoulders over anything else they saw."

"Well, I guess we'll wait and find out, won't we?"

He grinned at her. "My wife, the president of Hickston College. Will I still be allowed to call you Miranda?"

"Certainly not in public," she joked.

"Heavens, no. I mean when we're home alone."

"I suppose that would be acceptable, but please don't overdo it. I'll have a reputation to protect."

"I understand completely. Shall we eat now, Madame President?"

"Yes, we shall."

The hostess led them to a table for two with the best view of the Hudson, and they had scarcely settled into the chairs when the owner, Henri Legrand, came over bearing two glasses of champagne.

"What a privilege to have you with us celebrating your wedding," he said with an unmistakably French accent. "It was today, yes?"

"At 3:30 p.m.," Grant told him. "Just the two of us and Steinville's mayor."

"*Et nous sommes ravis de partager cette soirée avec vous,*" Miranda added. We're delighted to share this evening with you.

Any possibility that the dining experience might have been less than perfect ended when Henri heard Miranda's flawless French and, after a brief exchange in his native language, learned that her favorite French city was Lille. He immediately removed the two glasses of champagne and returned a minute later with a bottle of Dom Perignon and three glasses. The champagne and the dinner were on him, he insisted, owing to the *grande miracle* that the chairwoman of Hickston's French department thought that his hometown, Lille, was the finest city in all of France.

He toasted their marriage, their health, and the meal that he vowed would be *le meilleur de tous les temps.* The finest of all time.

They began by sharing a golden cheese soufflé so airy it almost floated from their forks to their mouths. Following the delicate appetizer, they both chose seafood entrées—Dover sole for her, Maine lobster for him. Finally, they shared two desserts, an apple tarte Tatin with Chantilly cream and classic French crème au caramel. As Henri had promised, it was without question a spectacular meal.

Before leaving, they told Henri about the party they would be having sometime that summer and asked whether he ever catered such events. He did so rarely, he said, and then only for family and close friends.

"And since you are now close friends," he added with a broad smile, "I will gladly do so for you. Simply call me well ahead of time so that we can agree on a date."

During the short ride home they marveled at what had turned out to be an unforgettable day. Despite her misgivings, Miranda had formally declared her interest in becoming Hickston's next president. Then, more or less on the spur of the moment, they had gotten married. Next, Withers had invited her to meet with the college's board of trustees the following morning. And, finally, the owner of their favorite restaurant had treated them to a meal that undoubtedly would have cost them four hundred dollars.

"Pretty full day," Grant said as they followed Route 218 south toward Steinville.

"A full day and a full *me*. I can't believe I ate that much."

"I think there's a law that says you're allowed to overeat on your wedding day."

"Ah, then I feel much better. All I have to do now is lie awake all night and think about meeting with the board tomorrow."

"You already know the answer to every question they can possibly ask," he assured her. "You're more than ready."

"But I'm still nervous."

"You're excited, not nervous. There's a difference."

"Feels the same to me."

"Yeah, I guess it does. But trust me, Miranda, you're going to kill the interview because you have a unique background. Think how long it would take for an outsider to learn what you already know about both Hickston and Steinville. You're a top academic as well as an elected official. Who can beat that?"

"We'll see."

"Yes, we will."

"In the meantime, we've both had enough excitement for one day, haven't we?"

"More than enough."

177

But the day's excitement was not quite over. They had just walked into the kitchen when Grant's cell phone rang, and he took a call from Hampton, Westbrook Publishing, one of the country's biggest names in romance fiction.

Executive Editor Victoria Zahn introduced herself as a Yale classmate of Georgette Mealey and asked Grant whether he had a moment to discuss his latest novel. He did, of course.

"I had lunch in Manhattan with Georgette several days ago," she said, "and she gave me a copy of your short story collection, which I thoroughly enjoyed. She also mentioned that you're working on a novel that might interest me."

"Yes, it's coming along nicely," he told her, "and I expect to finish it before classes begin in September."

"Could you tell me something about it?"

"Sure, I'd be happy to."

He gave her a quick overview of the plot and the main characters, noting that to his mind, at least, the story landed somewhere between *Sleepless in Seattle* and *Beauty and the Beast*, with an extra helping of humor thrown in.

"And a happy ending?" Victoria wondered.

"Deliriously happy, yes."

"I'd like to have the first look at it. Is that something you would do for Georgette's old classmate?"

It was the easiest decision of his life.

"Something good?" Miranda asked when the call ended.

"Almost too good to be true," he said before explaining what had just happened.

"My husband, the famous romance writer. Will I still be allowed to call you Grant?"

"Certainly not in public."

"No, of course not. I mean when we're home alone."

"I suppose that would be acceptable, but please don't overdo it. I'll have a reputation to protect."

For reasons they could not begin to fathom, the sun, moon, and stars had decided to align perfectly just for them.

They decided to discuss the issue further in bed.

45.

Miranda entered the boardroom a few minutes before 10:00 a.m. and shook hands with the seven men and four women who were about to assess her presidential qualities. She wore an expensive pearl gray pencil skirt, a matching jacket, and a tastefully elegant white silk blouse. On her left hand was a new white-gold wedding band, but no one seemed to notice or care. All the board wanted was someone who could grab the helm of a ship that was at risk of foundering in a financial tempest.

The meeting began with Withers at the head of the long mahogany table, five board members on each side, and Miranda at the far end opposite the chairman. All the members had been given an advance copy of the application package she had submitted, so they were already familiar with her background as well as her thoughts on where Hickston should be headed. The session opened, however, not with a discussion of her credentials but with Withers' summary of the theft that had led to Farnsworth's firing.

"In the interest of full disclosure," he began, "I must tell you that Hickston was recently the victim of a major theft that has left everyone in this room quite shaken. Have you heard anything about this?"

"I've heard a rumor that two million dollars was illegally transferred out of the college's bank accounts and that Professor Hannah Grackle was somehow implicated."

"What you heard is largely accurate, I'm afraid. Someone stole two million dollars, and our banks refuse to absorb the loss. As for Professor Grackle, the FBI does not believe she was an active participant in the scheme. But because she unwittingly gave someone access to Hickston's secure computer system, she had to be let go."

"Are all three banks local?" she asked. He nodded and named them. "Have you met with the bank presidents face to face?"

"I have not."

"I know all three presidents through my work on the town council," she observed, "and I can assure you those banks have a vested interest in Hickston's future. Simply put, if Hickston fails, Steinville fails. And if Steinville fails, those three banks will fold. I believe that if asked properly, they will cover the college's losses."

The conviction with which she delivered the pronouncement captured everyone's attention. Having grown accustomed to Farnsworth's constant hedging and buck-passing, the board found the boldness of her remarks refreshing.

"And you would be prepared to have such conversations if you were named president?" Withers asked.

"That's the first thing I would do, yes."

Satisfied with that response, the board asked her to describe the most important steps she would take to improve Hickston's fortunes. She addressed three core issues, expanding on ideas she had laid out in her written summary.

First, she would upgrade the quality of the student body. In her view, the college needed not just more students but better students. She had seen a steady decline in the aptitude and attitude of Hickston undergraduates in recent years, and she declared it was time to weed out the knuckle-draggers who majored in alcohol consumption.

"Our basketball program has given us extremely favorable national exposure that has not been leveraged," she said. "An effective advertising program would allow us to establish Hickston as both a basketball powerhouse and a college that is becoming increasingly selective. It's time we aspired to greatness as an academic institution."

Second, she would launch an aggressive internship program that placed Hickston students in local businesses as well as in participating New York City corporations. Students would gain real-world experience that burnished their resumes, she explained, while businesses would benefit from a steady supply of young talent. "We're a liberal arts college," she said, "but students still need jobs when they graduate. The program I have in mind will make Hickston one of the most desirable small colleges in America."

Third, she would replace the current do-nothing fundraising team in order to get serious about finding the big bucks Hickston needed in order to bolster its paltry endowment. "Among other things," she said sharply, "I would want a vice president for institutional advancement who doesn't require a putting green in his office."

Her comment raised eyebrows all around the table.

"Do you believe Arthur Sproull played golf in his office?" Withers asked, plainly appalled by the thought.

"I believe it because it's true." She took out her cell phone and showed him the picture Grant had taken in Sproull's office. "The person who took this photo said he was quite good, actually, but golf is not what he was being paid for."

The rigorous Q and A that followed ran until noon, at which time a team of servers arrived to set up a buffet lunch. Miranda nibbled while being peppered with questions about a wide range of subjects, everything from the shabbiness of Hickston's oldest buildings to the role a board of trustees should play in campus governance. Her answers reinforced the board's earlier assessment that she was someone who said only what she believed instead of what she thought her audience wanted to hear. This was a radical departure from the style of the former president, who said whatever got him through the moment even if he knew it wasn't true.

When lunch was over and the dishes had been cleared, Withers asked Miranda if she had any questions for the board.

"Only one," she said. "Do you have any idea how long it will take you to reach a decision once you've interviewed all the candidates?"

Withers looked around the table and smiled.

"Fairly quickly, I should think, since there are no other candidates." He caught the look on Miranda's face. "You're surprised, of course, but the fact is we rejected fifty-two other applications out of hand. Hickston doesn't have time for someone to come in and spend a few years getting to know the place. We need someone who can hit the ground running and make things happen immediately both on campus and in the local community."

He asked if she would mind stepping out of the room while the board members considered everything they had heard. When she stood to leave, he suggested that she stay close by. Seven minutes later she was welcomed back into the boardroom with a round of applause.

Miranda Davignon had just been named captain of the Titanic.

46.

Grant and Miranda couldn't decide which of them was more shocked by the speed with which things were moving, but they both held up well under the pressure. Grant stuck to a rugged schedule: two thousand words per day, seven days per week. At that pace he would deliver the manuscript of his first novel to Victoria Zahn before the start of the fall semester.

Miranda, meanwhile, began checking off the tasks she felt were most critical to Hickston's future. The day after being named president, she met with each of the three local bank presidents who had earlier refused to make the college whole following the two-million-dollar theft. She convinced them that Hickston and Steinville would either succeed together or fail together and that it was therefore in their own self-interest to cover the full loss.

All three banks restored the money to the college's accounts within twenty-four hours.

Then she hired Dana McArdle's advertising firm to create a national campaign that would use Hickston's basketball fame to remake the school's student body. Two weeks after the campaign's launch, applications were up sharply, and the admissions office was accepting only those students whose credentials met the higher standards of what Miranda called "the new Hickston."

Riding the success of the school's national ad campaign, the revamped fundraising team began asking for and receiving major contributions from wealthy alumni and friends as well as from businesses that had agreed to participate in Hickston's new highly acclaimed internship program. During July, normally a dead month for fundraising, the college logged gifts totaling six million dollars, eight times more than the previous one-month record.

Then came the bombshell. Following their grand August wedding in Israel, Naomi and Aaron sent Miranda a check for fifty million dollars in honor of her becoming Hickston's first female president. A small portion of the gift was earmarked for an endowed archaeology professorship bearing Naomi's name, but the remainder would be used at Miranda's discretion to upgrade facilities, strengthen the curriculum, and provide scholarships to top-tier students.

Tears of joy streamed down Miranda's face when she called Naomi and Aaron to thank them for the incredibly large gift, one that almost certainly would change Hickston's trajectory. But they brushed aside her concern that the gift was too large. Fifty million dollars was only a fraction of the annual earnings on the money Aaron's father had left him, they said, and they planned to be as generous as they could with their wealth because they had far more than they would ever need.

"Money follows money," Aaron told her. "When donors learn that someone has made a fifty-million-dollar gift to your college, other large gifts will follow. Naomi and I are glad to prime the pump for you."

The only break Grant and Miranda took from their busy schedules was the two-day period in late August when they moved out of the home they had purchased from Naomi and into the president's house on campus. They had wisely decided to rent their home to a young faculty couple rather than sell it outright. Since Miranda would not be Hickston's president forever, they would eventually need a place of their own. Whether that was ten weeks down the road or ten years was anyone's guess.

The campus mansion came fully furnished, of course, but Miranda described the decor as Early Axe Murderer. Using Hickston's funds, Farnsworth had spent lavishly to give Alicia Fillip the home of her dreams, a dark, cavernous place that struck the new president as part Gothic castle and part chamber of horrors.

All that was missing from the immense black-and-purple living room couch, Miranda joked, was a bloody corpse, and the hulking double-pedestal dining room table looked more like a medieval torture device than a place where family and friends might enjoy gathering. Adding a touch of Grim Reaper to every room in the house were shiny black drapes that efficiently blocked all sunlight from entering, as though the place had been occupied by vampires.

"I always considered Alicia a little odd," Miranda told Grant on the day the movers came to cart off all the old furniture and replace it with more welcoming and far less expensive stuff, "but I didn't suspect she was Dracula's bride."

Never one to waste resources, she sold all the old furnishings at a profit to a set design company in New York City, adding nearly one hundred thousand dollars to Hickston's coffers.

In virtually every way imaginable, the early days of Miranda's tenure as president went more smoothly than anyone could have expected. Until August 25th, that is, when Hickston's newly upgraded financial software detected simultaneous attacks on the college's three bank accounts. In addition to blocking the withdrawals, however, the new system generated a detailed report on the attempted breaches and automatically forwarded it to FBI Special Agents Jorge Suarez and Marla Kincaid, who thus far had been unsuccessful in locating Russian thief Oleg Gruzdev.

With a modest bit of effort and the full cooperation of the Serbian government, the FBI traced the failed transactions to a luxurious villa on the Danube in Belgrade, where Gruzdev was living comfortably with a ninety-year-old widow to whom he had recently become engaged. Had he succeeded in marrying her, he would have shared a fortune estimated at three hundred million dollars. Notably, at the time of his arrest by Serbian police, Gruzdev had in his possession a first-class ticket to Morocco, where he could have lived like a prince without the threat of extradition. But since the FBI claimed him first, he returned to the United States in the last row of an Air Serbia flight with a U.S. Marshal sitting next to him.

Agent Suarez was kind enough to call and let Miranda know that Gruzdev would reside in a federal detention center until his trial began.

"But I'm sorry to report that the money he stole from Hickston is long gone," he reported.

"Hidden?"

"Spent."

"It seems impossible to spend two million dollars so quickly."

"Not if you're Gruzdev," Suarez said seriously.

After stealing Hickston's money, Gruzdev had flown to Monaco by private jet, played blackjack for fifty thousand dollars a hand at the

Monte Carlo Casino, stayed at the Hôtel de Paris in a suite that cost thirty thousand dollars per night, and left town with barely enough money to cover the cost of a twenty-two-hour bus trip to Belgrade. When he needed some quick cash prior to marrying the old widow, he foolishly attempted to tap into Hickston's bank accounts one more time.

"What happens to him now?"

"He's facing a million-dollar fine and thirty years in prison, and that's only in the U.S. I suspect that as time goes on we'll learn he's wanted in other countries, so I doubt he'll ever be a free man again."

Miranda asked whether Suarez had heard anything about Hannah Grackle following her termination, and he said that the FBI had, in fact, kept tabs on her in case her testimony was required at trial. She was presently training to become a nun at a convent in a remote corner of Louisiana.

Suarez had it on good authority that the other nuns were already talking about taking Grackle on a midnight visit to an alligator ranch just up the highway.

185

47.

On August 29th, a week before the beginning of Hickston's fall semester, Grant took a deep breath, pushed ENTER, and emailed *The
Professors of Love* to Victoria Zahn. He had given the project his best
effort and now could only wait for her feedback.

During the final stages of the editing process, he had made the plot
change that Miranda had recommended in order to make the novel read
less like *Sleepless in Seattle*. Instead of having the female protagonist engaged to someone else, she and the male protagonist, both archaeology
professors, were happily unattached and wedded only to their careers. And
instead of meeting on a college campus, they met in the Negev Desert
while participating in an archaeological dig.

In other words, the novel had turned into the story of Naomi Perlmutter and Aaron Weiss, to whom the book was now dedicated. Naomi
and Aaron had eagerly given their blessing to the idea, asking only that
Grant give them different names. Thus they became Sharon and Jeremy,
two strangers who had fallen madly in love while helping each other lift
a clay pot from an ancient tomb.

After emailing the manuscript, Grant met Miranda for lunch at Vulture Commons, where a new food service was now responsible for
feeding Hickston's multitudes. With some trepidation, Grant ordered
the beef stew, formerly best known for containing brush bristles the size
of toothpicks, and was pleasantly surprised to learn that the new recipe
contained no potentially deadly objects. Miranda opted for grilled
chicken atop a salad that, in a refreshing change, was neither brown nor
wilted. The new food service was off to a good start.

"So how does it feel to have your novel in a publisher's hands?"
Miranda asked between bites.

"I'm nervous."

"You're excited, not nervous. Isn't that what you told me before my board interview?"

"I deny it completely," he said. "Actually, what I'm feeling is more fear than nervousness."

"A couple of months ago you had everything riding on this book. But now that you have tenure, the pressure is off. The novel doesn't need to be an instant success."

"True," he said, "but no writer wants to be rejected."

She locked eyes with him and shook her head gently.

"I think it would be better to talk about rejection only if Victoria actually rejects it."

"I guess."

"And, for the record, she's not going to reject it. I've read the draft, Grant, and it's really good. It's touching, it's funny, and it's real." She thought for a moment. "It would make a great movie. How many love stories are set in the Negev Desert?"

"I think we should hold off talking about the movie until someone actually publishes the novel."

She smiled. "Okay, we'll wait. But the movie will be wonderful."

Late that same evening, Victoria Zahn removed guesswork from the equation when she called Grant to say she had devoted her entire day to reading the manuscript. She believed it had just the right balance between tenderness, lust, and comedy, and she predicted it would be a huge hit once a few editorial changes had been made. Aside from moving a few paragraphs around and adjusting word choice here and there, she felt it was important to change the title.

"I don't think *The Professors of Love* captures the essence of the story," she told him. "I'd rather come up with something a little exotic that suggests love blooming in the desert. What do you think?"

"You're the expert. Whatever you think will help it sell is fine by me."

"Then I hope you won't be upset when I also suggest publishing this under a pen name."

"Why would I do that?"

"Because most romance authors are women, as are most of the readers. And some of the most successful male romance authors write under women's names. It's your call," Victoria added, "but the difference between your own name and a pseudonym might be several thousand copies."

"In that case, let's use a pseudonym. Do you have one in mind?"

"Tara Hemingway."

"Any relation to Ernest?"

"None."

"Okay, I'm in. What happens next?"

"You sit tight while I work a bit of editorial magic. After you sign off on the revisions, we'll print and begin shipping copies to bookstores. We'll start with twenty-five thousand copies and go from there."

And go from there they did. Early reviewers of *My Desert Love* were universally lavish in their praise, with one famous critic labeling it "the most impressive first novel of any genre" that she had read. On September 9th, as orders rocketed, Victoria authorized a second printing, this one for five hundred thousand copies. Even though most sales were for digital editions of the novel, the appetite for hardcover copies was enormous.

Never before in the long and glorious history of Hampton, Westbrook Publishing had a first novel by one of its authors made the *New York Times* bestseller list. A week after its release, *My Desert Love* was number one, and Grant was well on his way to banking his first million.

48.

On the Saturday before classes began, Miranda invited the entire Hickston faculty to a merry outdoor reception at the president's house. The only business item on the agenda was the formal announcement of the fifty-million-dollar gift from Naomi and Aaron. For the benefit of those who remembered Farnsworth's announcement of a forty-million-dollar gift that never materialized, she made a point of saying that the check had been cashed and that the money was already being invested by a team of professional portfolio managers.

"I do have one non-business item worth mentioning before I let you return to having fun," she said, beckoning Grant to join her in front of their guests. "I am pleased to confirm the rumor that I am married to Tara Hemingway, the author of *My Desert Love*, which is presently the top-selling book in America."

The only people who weren't confused by the announcement were Jim and Dana McArdle, who had already been let in on the secret. Everyone else looked lost.

"My editor decided a pen name was in order since most romance readers are women," Grant explained, "and Tara Hemingway is the name she came up with."

A biology professor near the back of the crowd raised her hand and shouted, "I love that book!" Other hands were raised and other words of praise offered. It quickly became clear that more than half the audience had read Grant's first novel.

After that, the afternoon was devoted to fine food and the sort of collegial atmosphere Hickston hadn't enjoyed for too long. There had always been an aloofness about Farnsworth that had rubbed faculty members the wrong way. He had seemed to believe that the college existed for the sake of the administration when, in fact, the administration existed solely for the sake of supporting the work of Hickston's faculty and students. Having one of their own take the reins was therefore a pivotal moment in the school's history, and everyone at the party sensed that big things were on the way.

A week later Grant and Miranda held a second reception, this one indoors and quite a bit smaller. The guests were family and friends who had gathered for lunch to celebrate the recent wedding as well as Miranda's new job and Grant's first novel. The elegant French meal was prepared and served by the staff of Les Bois, with owner Henri Legrand on hand to make sure everything was done to his exacting standards.

There were no speeches, but Grant offered a rousing impromptu toast to those who had conspired to make life wonderful for him and Miranda. He thanked Hannah Grackle for denying him tenure. If she hadn't done so, he would not have been desperate to write a novel, in which case Miranda would not have become his literary coach. He thanked Jim and Dana for sharing their Adirondack vacation home, without which he might never have dared to tell Miranda that he loved her. He thanked Naomi and Aaron, who had flown in for the occasion, for agreeing to become the stars of his first novel. And he offered special thanks to Porter Farnsworth, whose incompetence had made it possible for a Russian thief to steal two million dollars, thereby opening the door for Miranda to become Hickston's president.

At the same moment Grant was offering the toast, Farnsworth was sitting on the edge of his bed in a dreary North Dakota motel room wondering why Alicia Fillip wasn't answering the phone at their Manhattan apartment. He had interviewed late the day before for the presidency of Renville County Community College in Sherwood, N.D., a flyspeck of a town located three miles south of the Canadian border. The sixty-five-mile drive to Minot International Airport would take him a little over an hour if the dusting of September snow didn't slow him down.

Farnsworth had no particular desire to live and work where the winter temperature routinely fell to minus forty degrees, but Renville County CC was the only institution willing to have him meet with its presidential search committee. He had come to town with high hopes, believing he would be viewed as a larger-than-life figure, a higher-education rock star in the eyes of Sherwood's two hundred and seventeen full-time residents. But in a place where one of the major events on the cultural calendar was the annual fire department pancake breakfast, the Porter Farnsworth show didn't play well.

His five-thousand-dollar pinstripe suit gave him the appearance of an undertaker among board members attired in casual slacks and tieless shirts. And his intimidating Ivy League vocabulary made him sound like a snake oil salesman, something the folks of Sherwood didn't need or want. Having gotten off to a bumpy start, the interview abruptly ended after thirty minutes when the board chairman, a pious Sherwood minister, asked the candidate about his marital status and learned that Farnsworth had been living on the Hickston College campus "in carnal sin," as the minister put it, with "a shameless harlot."

The harlot in question, Farnsworth would soon learn, was not answering the phone back in New York because she had recently reconnected with an old beau who was employed by one of the country's premier investment banks. He was newly divorced, eager for the sort of companionship Alicia had been famous for in college, and rich beyond his wildest dreams. His thirty-million-dollar home in East Hampton seemed like the sort of place Alicia could get used to, especially if he was open-minded about a little redecorating.

After departing Sherwood for Minot, Farnsworth got a speeding ticket as he passed through Glenburn while doing sixty-eight in a sixty-five zone. His abysmal luck continued when he boarded what should have been a five-hour, one-stop flight to Newark Liberty. The trip actually lasted nearly twelve hours after he missed his connection in Minneapolis. When he reached Newark at 3:15 a.m., he discovered that his car had been stolen from the long-term lot. He filed a report with the Newark police, then spent seventy-five dollars on a cab ride to Manhattan, where he wearily rode the elevator to his third-floor apartment.

He found Alicia's handwritten note on his pillow.

Hope the interview went well. I'm in love with someone else and trust you'll understand. All the best, Alicia.

Exhausted and disgusted, he was in no mood for what he believed was Alicia's poor attempt at humor.

Then he opened the door of her empty closet.

49.

On November 9th the Hickston Vultures men's basketball team began its quest for a third consecutive national championship with a 98-63 victory over Kansas in Madison Square Garden. Winston Churchill Mbongo, the seven-foot-eight All-American who had once again shocked the sports world by not turning pro, scored thirty-three points in the first half. After scoring another ten early in the second half, he asked Coach Tex Brawner to take him out of the game because he didn't want to humiliate the opposing players.

Three nights later, a Saturday, the Vultures opened their home season with President Miranda Davignon and Associate Professor Grant Hunter sitting side by side in the stands at midcourt. Miranda could have had any seats she wanted, of course, but Grant wanted to use the season tickets Tex had given him the previous spring.

The Vultures won 115-67 over Bryant University, with Winston scoring a game-high forty-eight points. He spent almost the entire second half rebounding and setting up his teammates rather than taking shots, once again choosing not to offend the visitors by scoring as many points as he could have. This was his style. If the opposing players were friendly and respectful, as most were, he played only hard enough to make sure his team won. On those rare occasions when an opponent talked trash or played dirty, he was more than willing to pull out all the stops.

The day after the Bryant game, Tex and Sherry Brawner came to the president's house for lunch, bringing with them son Brad, who a few days earlier had celebrated his first birthday. He was an active toddler who had been walking for three months already, which meant that nothing in the home escaped his interest or his grasp. But Tex and Sherry were able to relax because Grant and Miranda were having a fine time playing with him. Brad was tall for his age, thirty-three inches, and Grant pronounced him a future Hickston All-American.

"I was a little nervous about bringing Brad here today," Sherry said to Miranda when the two men went outside to play something resembling soccer with their younger teammate. "He sort of gets into everything."

"We love having him here," Miranda assured her, "and we'll gladly serve as Brad's unofficial aunt and uncle. I hope the three of you will be here often."

"You've done a wonderful job with this place, by the way. The last time I was here it looked like a funeral parlor. Why do you suppose Alicia Fillip decorated it that way?"

"Grant claims he saw her turn into a bat once, but I assume he was joking." Sherry laughed so hard she nearly spilled her ginger ale. "Are you sure I can't interest you in a glass of wine?" Miranda asked.

Sherry shook her head slightly and grinned. "No alcohol for the next eight months."

Outside, meanwhile, Brad was chasing a squirrel up a tree when Tex waved to a large, beefy guy who was walking past the president's house with his girlfriend. The young woman's immense belly suggested that she and her boyfriend had been doing more than holding hands.

"I know those two," Grant said. "In fact, I had a fairly unpleasant experience with both of them."

"Not surprising. They both got a little shortchanged when common sense was being handed out," Tex noted. "Neander Slunk was a decent linebacker until he flunked out last year, but not before getting Juliet Swanson pregnant. I think it's safe to assume this is her final semester."

Karma was the first word that popped into Grant's head, but he dropped the thought when Miranda came to the side door and announced that lunch was ready: coq au vin for the adults, homemade chicken nuggets with mac and cheese for Brad. The adults talked while Brad devoted his full attention to the food on his high chair tray.

"The new season is off to an amazing start," Grant said. "Miranda and I watched the Kansas game on TV, and Winston was his usual spectacular self. It's incredible he's still here, isn't it?"

"Not really," Tex answered. "He grew up in a hut in a tiny Cameroon village, and money doesn't matter much to him. All he cares about is earning a college degree and helping his team win another national championship. He loves Hickston."

"And how about you?" Miranda wondered. "Are you happy here? I'm sure all the big universities are after you now."

He nodded. "They are, and I've said no to ten or twelve already. But it's Winston they want, not me. They'd hire me if Winston agreed to transfer, and then I'd be spare change as soon as he graduated. Sherry and I are happy right here. It's too bad coaches don't have tenure."

"There's a way around that, you know." He looked puzzled. "We can have you appointed a tenured associate professor of exercise science and physical education. That way if some future president no longer wants you as coach, you'll still be here."

"Is that a formal offer?" he asked.

"It is."

"I accept."

Grant interrupted the business deal with, "And now for our ulterior motive in having you here for lunch today."

"*His* ulterior motive," Miranda corrected. "But I fully endorse the idea."

The idea, Grant explained, was to have Tex and Sherry serve as the protagonists of his next novel. Their names would change, naturally, but the story would mirror their own. A young basketball coach meets the young alumni director, and they quickly fall in love. Grant had already been given a fat advance on the second novel, and the outline was ready to go.

"Will it be happy and funny?" Sherry asked.

"Just like *My Desert Love*. Same basic plot, different characters."

"Then I vote yes."

"As long as you put some basketball in it," Tex added, "I'm fine with the idea. Plus, Sherry and I each get a free book."

"We have a deal," Grant said. "But I charge for autographs."

After lunch, Brad napped on the couch while the adults talked about anything but business. There was no need.

Things could not have been better at Hickston College.

50.

The sunroom stretched from the back of the house toward a quiet cove that had been iced over for several days. The two side walls, mostly glass, offered unobstructed views of Lake George and the surrounding forest. At the far end of the room two tall windows stood on either side of a massive stone fireplace where five oak logs successfully kept winter's chill at bay.

Grant and Miranda had closed on their vacation home at the end of November, and this was their first time entertaining. It had taken the guests thirty minutes to drive there, but in summer they would be able to make the trip faster by boat since they lived directly across the lake from their newest neighbors.

Jim and Dana relaxed on an oversized beige couch that faced their home on the opposite shore. Their hosts sat across from them on cushioned wicker chairs that had been in the same spot since the home's previous owners had put them there twenty-five years earlier. Grant and Miranda had bought the place fully furnished for seven hundred thousand dollars, but they hadn't needed a mortgage because Grant's royalties on *My Desert Love* had already topped three-quarters of a million. Readers had fallen in love with Tara Hemingway, and they were panting for her next book.

"We're thinking of getting a telescope for the sunroom," Grant joked, "so that we can keep an eye on you two across the lake."

"If you look closely enough," Jim replied nonchalantly, "you'll see that our telescope is already in place. Attached to a camera, of course."

Miranda rolled her eyes. "Do adult males always turn into little boys when you bring them to a lake house?" she asked Dana.

"Sorry to burst your bubble, Miranda. *Adult male* is an oxymoron."

"Careful," Jim said. "We're only thirteen days away from Christmas, and you don't want Santa shortchanging you."

"If Santa shortchanges me," she countered, faking a sneer, "he'll be sleeping on a cot in the garage."

The conversation eventually turned to the true purpose for the happy gathering: Miranda's forty-second birthday. She and Grant had expected to mark the occasion alone but were delighted to learn that Jim and Dana would also be at their lake house for the weekend. The only issue yet to be resolved was where they would all be having dinner. Some of their favorite restaurants were closed during the winter months, but Grant had told Miranda not to worry.

He had a surprise in store.

The surprise began at 4:30 p.m., when Miranda saw a white van emerge from the trail behind their home. The driver parked near the kitchen door.

"Are you expecting someone?" she asked Grant.

"No," he said. "I'm expecting a couple of someones. Let's all go say hello."

The four of them greeted the two new arrivals, who introduced themselves as Pierre and Hélène Legrand. Both were wearing white chef jackets.

"You know my older brother, Henri," Pierre told Miranda in heavily accented English.

"You mean from Les Bois?"

"*Exactement.* Hélène and I own a restaurant in Killington, Vermont, and we have come here to prepare a very special birthday dinner for you and your guests."

Miranda turned to Grant in disbelief. "How could you possibly arrange something like this?"

"I didn't. Henri did. I told him I wanted to do something special for your birthday, and he said Pierre and Hélène might be willing to help."

"It's not a long drive," Hélène said offhandedly. "Less than an hour and a half to get here. *C'est notre plaisir.*" It's our pleasure.

Grant and Jim insisted on helping carry everything in from the van—coolers of food, bottles of wine, and a collection of professional cookware—and the chefs graciously accepted. But then with a wave of his hand Pierre ordered the four diners from the kitchen so that he and his wife could begin preparing a meal worthy of royalty.

As the amazing aromas of French food found their way to the sunroom, Grant set up his laptop and announced Miranda's second birthday present. He had booked a week in July at a magnificent eighteenth-century villa in Provence. The four of them settled onto the couch to watch a five-minute video, set to an orchestral version of Debussy's "Clair de Lune," that showcased a seven-bedroom, seven-bath hilltop home nestled among fields of lavender. The home's interior, measuring nearly five thousand square feet, featured immense open spaces and elegant high-end furnishings. The exterior offered a heated pool, a covered dining area, and stone paths that meandered through lush gardens.

When the video ended, Miranda turned to Grant, obviously confused.

"It's a bed and breakfast, right? We have one bedroom?"

"No, we have the entire villa. We can sleep in a different bedroom every night, if you'd like."

"The entire villa?"

"Yes."

"In Provence?"

"Bonnieux, yes, which Henri tells me is one of the most beautiful towns in Provence. It's about an hour-and-a-half drive to Marseille and, notably, an hour to Avignon, which I assume is where the Davignon family got its name a very long time ago."

"This is too extravagant, Grant."

"I respectfully disagree. It's part birthday present, part honeymoon, and part celebration of your becoming Hickston's president. And you don't need to check your calendar," he added, "because your secretary has already cleared that week for you."

"Then I guess I'm stuck going to Provence."

"I guess you are."

She wrapped her arms around his neck just as Hélène arrived to announce that dinner was about to be served.

"*Après le baiser, bien sûr,*" Hélène added with a smile. After the kiss, of course.

Dinner was served in the dining room on a table covered with crisp white linen the chefs had brought with them for the occasion. First up was a wonderful goat cheese tart with mushrooms and truffle oil. Then came the *pièce de résistance,* a stunning bouillabaisse featuring shelled Maine lobster. And for dessert Pierre and Hélène served a tasting menu of crème brûlée, sour cherry galette, and chocolate mousse.

Following the lavish meal, the diners finished their coffee in the sunroom while Pierre and Hélène put the kitchen back in order and got ready for the drive home. Thirty minutes later, Grant and Miranda saw the chefs off at the kitchen door with hugs and a solemn promise to visit the Vermont restaurant frequently whenever they were at Lake George.

Miranda whispered a question to Grant before returning to the sunroom.

"It's your present to use as you wish," he answered.

"But do you like the idea?"

"I think it's a great idea."

"It's a really big place."

"It's a huge place."

"Then we agree?"

He nodded. "We do."

Miranda waited until Grant had loaded a few more logs into the fireplace before extending the invitation to Jim and Dana.

"If you two can get away for a week next July," she said, "Grant and I would love to have you stay with us in Provence."

Dana's jaw dropped. "Are you serious?"

"Absolutely. I think we'll have a great time together."

Dana turned to Jim to see how he felt about the idea.

"Unfortunately," Jim deadpanned, "I don't believe the villa has a basketball court."

"But there are plenty of restaurants and wineries," Grant noted. "And besides, the way you play, you should count yourself lucky there's no basketball court."

"Of course, we could leave these two home," Miranda said to Dana, who had just been thinking the same thing.

"Does anyone want to see the video again?" Grant asked.

The vote was unanimous. This time they watched on the seventy-inch living room TV as light snow began falling over Lake George.

It was seventeen degrees outside, but at that moment all they were thinking about was a sunlit hillside in the south of France.

51.

Grant and Miranda spent Christmas Eve with his parents in Lehigh, Pennsylvania, then drove to Hartwick, New York, on Christmas Day to stay overnight with her parents. Then they were off to Lake George for a winter getaway while the Hickston campus was quiet.

The two-hour drive to the lake was delayed by an obligatory stop in Cooperstown at the National Baseball Hall of Fame and Museum, a place Grant had always wanted to visit. It was only a fifteen-minute ride from the home where Miranda had grown up, and she had been there at least a dozen times with her father before going off to college.

Grant was standing in front of a protective case staring reverently at a 1952 Mickey Mantle Topps card worth seven million dollars. He had collected baseball cards as a kid but never anything worth more than the few cents he had paid.

"I can't believe you visited this place whenever you felt like it," he said, plainly in awe of his surroundings.

"Correction: whenever *my father* felt like it. He's even nuttier about baseball than you are."

"Excellent. He and I can watch some games together when your parents are at the lake house with us this summer."

"I'll be sure to have plenty of beer and peanuts on hand."

"Thanks."

"I was being sarcastic."

"I was pretending not to notice."

For Miranda's sake, Grant limited the visit to one hour, and then they were on their way to Lake George. Since it was nearly 4:00 when they arrived, they went right to the sunroom, got the fireplace going, and settled in as sunset turned the sky crimson and lavender above the treetops.

The first innocent flakes began falling before they went to bed that night, and by morning they were on their way to getting eighteen inches of snow. In addition to transforming Lake George into a picture post-card, the snow allowed them to spend the next five days exploring the woods on cross-country skis and snowshoes. Other than that, they re-laxed by the fire, read, and went out for lunch or dinner once the roads had been plowed.

There was, however, some work to be done. Miranda had vowed to "reinvigorate" Grant's French conversational skills, which had been de-ficient even in the best of times. He resisted at first, arguing that she could do all the talking in Provence, but she convinced him he needed to be able to function on his own.

"Imagine you want to drive into town and buy us some *viennoiseries* for breakfast at the local boulangerie," she said, "but you mistakenly or-der *viande roussie*. Instead of pastries, we would have scorched meat."

"Why would I go to the boulangerie without you?"

"Because you're a big boy."

"Debatable. And I'm sure the people at the boulangerie will speak English anyway."

"In Paris, possibly. In Bonnieux, doubtful. Most French people don't speak English."

He grinned. "Then I can just point at what I want."

"Chimpanzees are allowed to point at what they want," she countered, "but travelers living in a marvelous eighteenth-century villa are not."

So the lessons began, and by the third afternoon Grant's long-ig-nored French vocabulary began returning slowly. It was painfully obvious to both of them, though, that his sloppy pronunciation would require a full seven months of practice. He was learning once again that small differences in sound can make big differences in meaning. For ex-ample, his *partager*, to share, still sounded like *potager*, or vegetable garden. And *patois*, or dialect, sounded suspiciously like *putois*, or pole-cat. Miranda could only imagine the odd looks he would get in France if his grasp of the language didn't improve.

The outside world intruded on their winter holiday only twice, both times on the morning of New Year's Eve. First was a call from Miranda's secretary. She had opened a letter from Columbia University, Miranda's alma mater, asking her to be its next commencement speaker and to accept an honorary Doctor of Letters degree. Then came the call from Grant's editor, Victoria, telling him he was being offered a quarter of a million dollars for the film rights to *My Desert Love.*

They both said yes.

That night they watched the ball drop on Times Square, toasted each other, and shared the first kiss of the new year.

"Here's hoping the new year is even half as good as the one that just ended," Grant said as he held Miranda close. "Things have been so good it's actually a little scary, isn't it?"

She shook her head. "Some things are obviously meant to be."

After a momentary pause he said, " *We* were meant to be."

"*Je suis d'accord,*" she whispered.

"You want me to buy you a Honda Accord."

"No, Grant. *Je suis d'accord.* It means I agree!"

"Ah, of course."

"And now I think it's time we went to bed."

"*Je suis d'accord,*" he said with a sly smile. "*Mais pas pour dormir.*" But not to sleep.

On this they agreed *complètement.*

EPILOGUE

Shortly after leading the Vultures to a third consecutive NCAA championship—103-87 over the Baylor Bears—Winston Churchill Mbongo once again broke the hearts of NBA coaches by announcing he would return for his senior year of college. He was leaning toward attending medical school once he earned his undergraduate degree, but he reserved the right to play a few years of professional basketball first. One thing that would never change, though, was his desire to share his good fortune and help the people of Cameroon enjoy better lives. That, he told everyone, was his true calling.

Hickston's third national championship came at roughly the same time Hannah Grackle was being invited to leave the Louisiana convent where she had established herself as what the mother superior termed "the most disruptive force, aside from the 1918 flu pandemic, ever to afflict our loving community." She was given a choice: a one-way bus ticket to an American city of her choosing or an opportunity to swim with the inhabitants of the nearby alligator ranch. She opted for a ticket to Orlando, Florida, where she landed a job as a Walt Disney World costume character, roaming the grounds in alternating roles as Clarabelle Cow, Clara Cluck, and Dumbo.

As much as she detested the job, especially on brutally hot days when her heavy costume felt like a sauna, she was better off than Porter Farnsworth and Arthur Sproull, who had adjoining cells at the Wallkill Correctional Facility in southern New York State. Both had been tried and found guilty of felony conspiracy for doctoring Beatrice Hagfeldt's will and would spend the next seven years behind bars. Sproull devoted himself to a novel about a college fundraiser who wins the U.S. Open Championship by ten strokes over runner-up Tiger Woods. Farnsworth spent his time assisting the superintendent in designing a new fitness center for inmates. This marked the first time Farnsworth had actually applied his Ph.D. in recreation management to the real world, and he sensed the beginning of a new career.

Back in Steinville, meanwhile, Neander and Juliet Slunk and their six-month-old son Monk were still living with Juliet's parents. Neander worked part-time at a local Sunoco station while finishing auto mechanic school, and Juliet took online classes toward her Hickston degree. Unfortunately, Juliet had to drop her classes when the morning sickness became unbearable. She planned to resume her online education right after daughter Sheena was born.

All of this was happening in America while Rajah, the handsome Bengal cat, was continuing to adjust nicely to his comfortable new home in Tel Aviv. Shortly after arriving, he had made the acquaintance of a local resident, a Cairo spiny mouse, of which there were millions.

Rajah quickly learned that he couldn't eat just one.

Made in United States
Orlando, FL
28 April 2022

17283532R00126